The magic of Paris...

"Look," he said softly, pointing over and up.

Nicole followed his gaze. There, rising in the air, so close it seemed almost larger than life, was the angular metal skeleton of the Eiffel Tower. White lights picked out its every curve and strut, making it stand out against the dark sky.

"Oh!" she gasped in surprise. "It's—it's beautiful!"

She had seen the Eiffel Tower many times, of course—it was difficult to go anywhere in the center of Paris without coming upon yet another view of it. But from this angle it looked like a whole new structure, looming and strangely mysterious, almost alive.

Becoming aware that Luc was watching her rather than the Tower, she turned and met his gaze.

He smiled. "I thought you would appreciate it," he said. "You, I think, have the ability to see what is special, what is important."

His face moved closer. Nicole stared into his eyes, mesmerized by the guileless, undemanding appreciation she saw there. So different from the way Nate looked at her most of the time.

She did nothing to stop Luc as he bent down and kissed her. His lips felt soft and warm against her own, and she let her eyes fall shut as she pressed against him.

STUDENTS ACROSS
S.A.S.S.
THE SEVEN SEAS

Pardon My French

Cathy Hapka

speak
An Imprint of Penguin Group (USA) Inc.

SPEAK
Published by the Penguin Group
Penguin Group (USA) Inc.,
345 Hudson Street, New York, New York 10014, U.S.A.
Penguin Group (Canada), 90 Eglinton Avenue East, Suite 700, Toronto, Ontario, Canada M4P 2Y3
(a division of Pearson Penguin Canada Inc.)
Penguin Books Ltd, 80 Strand, London WC2R 0RL, England
Penguin Ireland, 25 St Stephen's Green, Dublin 2, Ireland
(a division of Penguin Books Ltd)
Penguin Group (Australia), 250 Camberwell Road, Camberwell, Victoria 3124, Australia
(a division of Pearson Australia Group Pty Ltd)
Penguin Books India Pvt Ltd, 11 Community Centre, Panchsheel Park,
New Delhi - 110 017, India
Penguin Group (NZ), Cnr Airborne and Rosedale Roads, Albany, Auckland 1310,
New Zealand (a division of Pearson New Zealand Ltd)
Penguin Books (South Africa) (Pty) Ltd, 24 Sturdee Avenue, Rosebank, Johannesburg 2196,
South Africa

Registered Offices: Penguin Books Ltd, 80 Strand, London WC2R 0RL, England

Published by Speak, an imprint of Penguin Group (USA) Inc., 2005

5 7 9 10 8 6 4

Interior art and design by Jeanine Henderson. Text set in Imago Book.

LIBRARY OF CONGRESS CATALOGING-IN-PUBLICATION DATA
Hapka, Cathy.
Pardon my French / by Cathy Hapka.
p.   cm. — (S.A.S.S.: Students Across the Seven Seas)
Summary: Seventeen-year-old Nicole's dreams and plans center around her boyfriend,
but a semester in Paris encourages her to think about herself and her future in a new way.
ISBN 978-0-14-240459-1
[1. Self-confidence—Fiction. 2. Foreign study—Fiction. 3. Schools—Fiction.
4. France—Fiction.] I. Title. II. Series.
PZ7.H1996Par 2005 [Fic]—dc22 2005043444

Printed in the United States of America

Pardon My French

Jardin des Tuileries

Paris Sewer Museum

Eiffel Tower

Nicole's Paris

Georges Pompidou Center
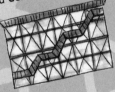

Cimetière du Père Lachaise

Louvre

Stravinsky Fountain

Seine

Notre Dame

Musée d' Orsay

Catacombes

Application for the Students Across the Seven Seas
Study Abroad Program

Name: Nicole Larson

Age: 17

High School: Peabody High School

Hometown: Peabody Corner, MD

Preferred Study Abroad Destination: Paris, France

1. Why are you interested in traveling abroad next year?

Answer: I would like to explore a different culture and learn how other people live. I would also enjoy learning in a new environment and studying a variety of subjects.

(Truth: I'm not interested at all. My parents have this obsessive need for me to expand my horizons, whatever that means.)

2. How will studying abroad further develop your talents and interests?

Answer: I believe my experiences in France will make me a more well-rounded person, which will help in my college application process and throughout my life.

(Truth: Are you kidding? I'll be lucky if I survive all the horizon expanding with my sanity intact! I mean, it's not as if I'm looking for any help in the beret-wearing or croissant-eating departments....)

3. Describe your extracurricular activities.

Answer: National Honor Society, Pep Squad, Yearbook.

(Truth: Nate, Nate, and more Nate. Oh, with a side order of shopping, gossiping with my three best friends, and pizza.)

4. Is there anything else you feel we should know about you?

Answer: I am a self-motivated student who will blossom in the S.A.S.S. program. I enjoy cooking, movies, and tennis.

(Truth: I would give my left arm NOT to be picked for the program.)

Chapter One

Dear Mom and Dad,

    You told me to send you a postcard to let you know when I got to Paris. So that's what I'm doing.

    I don't know what the building in the picture on the front is supposed to be, since AS YOU KNOW I don't speak or read French. At all.

    But luckily, you were right—I survived the flight. Barely.

    Anyway, weather's adequate, wish you were here...instead of me.

    —Nicole

• • •

"Are you sure we're going the right way?"

In the dirty rearview mirror, Nicole Larson saw the ruddy-faced taxi driver glance back at her. *"Oui, mademoiselle,"* he said, his cigarette dangling from his lower lip. His eyes were bloodshot; Nicole wondered if it was true what Zara had told her, that all Frenchmen drank a bottle of wine every morning for breakfast.

Maybe I should've mentioned that to Mom and Dad, she thought idly. *Warned them about the dangers of shipping an impressionable youth like me off to Paris, where it's like a nationwide frat party all the time. Explained that their only daughter could come home a hopeless drunk, all washed up at just seventeen years old.*

She sighed and leaned back against the seat, knowing that it wouldn't have made any difference. Her parents were determined that she was going to have a "learning experience" this fall even if it killed her. And of course they probably considered it a major bonus that Nate wasn't there.

Closing her eyes, Nicole did her best to conjure up a vision of her boyfriend's face. Nate Carlton: tall, broad-shouldered, greenish gray eyes, one somewhat crooked tooth that made his smile look slightly rakish, dirty-blond hair with just enough curl to make him look a little like an Abercrombie model. Even after almost two years together, Nicole still occasionally caught herself wondering, *Why me? How did I land a boyfriend like Nate?*

It wasn't that she'd ever had trouble attracting male attention, not even in her early middle-school years when her family was still moving a lot. Nicole knew she was lucky in that way, with her tall, slim figure, her wheat-blond hair, dimples, and almond-shaped hazel eyes. And she was grateful for it. She figured her looks were probably the only thing that had saved her from a life of desperate loneliness during the years she'd spent walking into one brand-new classroom after another, forcing herself to swallow back her fear and smile at yet another roomful of strangers as they stared and decided whether to accept her, ignore her, or make her life a living hell.

In that sense, she and Nate were perfectly matched—a "cute couple," as most people said. But Nate was about more than just good looks. He had the whole package. Funny, outgoing, the life of the party—anywhere Nate went, a good time usually followed. He had a way of making everyone around him loosen up and have fun. When he looked into Nicole's eyes, she forgot all of her anxieties and fears and just let herself be swept up in his energy.

That would have been enough for her. But there was even more—the Carlton money, for one thing. Nate's family might not be Rockefellers, but by the standards of Peabody Corner, Maryland, they were close enough. He was smart, too, and ambitious, and athletic. Even though he liked to tell everyone he was considering a pro football career after college, Nate already had "successful lawyer"

written all over him; his father and uncle probably had an office picked out for him in their luxurious building on Main Street. In other words, Nate was exactly the kind of guy Zara and Annie would label DTHB: Don't Throw Him Back.

Lucky. Lucky-lucky-lucky. How many times had Zara and the others said it? Nicole was lucky to have a guy like Nate. But now she was stuck spending the next three months far away from him in Croissantland. It didn't seem fair. She was supposed to spend the first semester of her senior year in a very different sort of way. She'd imagined it so many times, in such vivid detail. She could see herself walking through the halls with her friends whispering snarky, clever comments about the unfortunate fashion choices of the incoming freshmen. Cheering Nate on at the homecoming game, then leaning into him as they danced later that night. Staying up late with Annie "helping" her write an essay that might actually, miraculously, get her into college.

College. That was the main reason Nicole was here and she knew it. She stared down at her hands, trying not to let her mind go spinning down that familiar path. She was feeling depressed enough already.

The warm air blowing in through the half-open cab windows carried the sour, stale stench of cigarette smoke into the backseat. Nicole held her breath, trying not to let her distaste show on her face. If French people were half as touchy and rude as everyone back home said they were, she didn't want to take any chances of insulting the driver by making faces at his cancer breath. Besides, at this point she just wanted to get through this ride without having a complete nervous breakdown.

"Merde!" the driver muttered loudly, swerving violently around a small, scruffy-looking brown-and-white dog. Nicole tensed, clutching the armrest.

"Uh, don't worry," she spoke up tentatively. "I'm really not in a hurry."

The driver glanced at her again in the rearview. Nicole wondered if he spoke English at all. Maybe the only phrase he understood was "Do you speak English?" Or maybe his nod at this earlier question had been a fluke—maybe he'd just been shaking himself awake. Back at the airport, he had stared at the address she'd showed him, then merely jerked his head to indicate for her to follow him to his car. She still wasn't entirely convinced he knew where he was going, though it wasn't as if she could really tell the difference.

She looked out the window. *So this is Paris*, she thought.

She had been doing her best to ignore the scenery outside for as long as possible. Sooner or later, though, she would have to climb out of this cab and face the fact that she was here, in a foreign country where she didn't speak the language, all alone.

"Thanks, Mom and Dad," she muttered.

"Eh?" The cabdriver glanced back at her again.

"Nothing," Nicole said quickly, wincing as he nearly sideswiped a parked car.

Even though Zara was who-even-knew-how-many miles away, Nicole could almost hear her snicker. *Talking to yourself again, Larson?* Zara would say with that little twisted half smile of hers. *They have medication for that, you know.*

Annie and Patrice would giggle along, and even though Nicole would laugh, too—maybe even make some additional little joke at her own expense—she would end up feeling ashamed, as if she'd broken some kind of unwritten rule of proper behavior. One of Zara's favorite sayings was "Never let them see you sweat." She used it so much that she'd long since shorthanded it to NLTSYS, pronounced "Neltsiss."

Nicole's friendship with Zara, Annie, and Patrice was, like her relationship with Nate, a cherished symbol of how her life had finally eased into stability and predictability. It had begun in the middle of eighth grade, when her family had finally settled down—for good this time, her parents had promised—in Peabody Corner. First she'd found Patrice Fiorelli, bonding with her over their shared love of sappy romance novels. Then, that summer at the community pool, the unthinkable had happened—Zara Adams had actually shown an interest in her. And where Zara went, Annie Goodfellow followed; the two of them had been best friends practically since birth. They'd both been outrageously popular since birth, too, as far as Nicole could tell. When they folded her into their circle of friendship, along with Patrice, it was as if she'd suddenly graduated from character actor to leading lady. By the time they started high school that fall, the four of them were inseparable.

Nicole loved the feeling of being part of a group. Loved it so much that she didn't really mind that Zara made most of their plans, decided which after-school activities and hobbies were worthwhile, even picked out what clothes everyone should buy when they went to the mall. Most of the time Nicole completely agreed with her choices, anyway. Even when she didn't, it just seemed easier to go along with whatever Zara wanted.

And then came Nate. Landing him was one of the few things Nicole had ever done that she could tell truly impressed Zara. That felt good.

But even better was the feeling that in the past few years, finally, Nicole's life had gotten under control. No more moving. No more loneliness. She was safe—heading in just the right direction. She'd always imagined herself living in one of those romances she liked so much—a handsome, successful husband, a couple of adorable, loving children, a nice house in a nice neighborhood, a neatly tended yard with a cute Labrador retriever frolicking in the tulips....

Nicole always felt a little sheepish at the thought of telling people—especially her parents—about these soft-focus dreams, as if she ought to have bigger goals, like saving the rain forest or landing a spot on the Supreme Court. She frustratingly suspected her parents were just liberal and adventurous enough not to get it. Why else would they have spent her entire childhood cheerfully and carelessly uprooting their entire lives every year or so, just so they could design and install yet another public garden or private estate grounds?

But maybe it had been a bad move to keep it from them. Maybe if she'd tried to explain her dreams to them, they would have realized how much they were messing up her life by shipping her off to Paris just when she'd finally thought everything was settled. She had offered to rent French movies, listen to some French music, even try to survive dinner at a French restaurant, as long as they let her stay home where she belonged. But no; they wanted her to experience the real thing. Why couldn't they realize that she didn't care about travel and adventure, or about expanding her horizons? Her horizons were just fine the way they were.

Nicole stared out the window. It was a sunny September day, and there were plenty of people on the sidewalks and plenty of cars and trucks on the streets. While the people didn't appear that different from the ones back home, most of the vehicles looked strange and unfamiliar—tiny, boxy automobiles that looked more like kiddie cars than anything an adult would drive. The vans and delivery trucks looked more ordinary except that most of them had French names or phrases painted on their sides. At least the stop signs seemed to be the same in Paris as they were back home—they were even written in English.

They turned down a block of what Nicole guessed might be houses or apartment buildings, most of them three or four stories tall. The facades were as different from the spacious, brick-face–and–stucco homes in her subdivision back home in Maryland as the minicars were from Nate's enormous American-made SUV. These buildings were mostly constructed of various shades of gray stone and seemed to loom inches from the curb. Most of them looked as if they'd been squatting there, gray and solid and dusty, since dinosaurs roamed the earth.

Several people were strolling down the street, appearing to be in no hurry. Two young women wearing chic dresses were chatting with each other. A young boy was leaning out of a window watering flowers in a window box. A stout woman with a brightly colored scarf tied over her hair was sweeping the sidewalk.

Nicole stared out at the strangers, feeling a little like a naturalist observing wild animals in their native habitat from the safety of a Jeep. There was just one difference. Unlike a naturalist, she was going to have to live among the subjects of her observation. The thought made her

stomach twist with anxiety, and she swallowed hard as she felt the baked chicken and mashed potatoes she'd eaten on the plane—the last safe, familiar food she was likely to see for months—rise up into her throat. Tightening her grip on the armrest, she stared straight ahead until she felt her churning stomach subside a little.

The cabbie spun the steering wheel to the left and peeled off down another street. The residential area quickly gave way to what seemed to be a shopping area. There were many more people on the street, and most of the buildings had signs out front along with picture windows displaying their wares. Nicole noticed that many of them featured pictures indicating what was sold inside—a pair of shoes on a shoe-store sign, a cow on the sign for a butcher, a book in front of a bookstore.

Good, Nicole thought. *Guess that's how they keep the clueless Americans from bothering them with too many questions.*

Nicole leaned back and closed her eyes. Why oh why did she have to be stuck in France, of all places? If her parents insisted on shipping her off somewhere, why couldn't they have found a semester-abroad program in, like, Canada—or better yet, New Jersey? At least then she could speak the language and maybe have seen Nate on weekends.

But no, it had to be Paris. She was already enrolled in Introduction to French, a language-immersion course that promised to get her conversing with the locals in no time. Luckily the program's other courses were all taught in English—math, history, literature, even something called Paris Through an Artist's Eye.

Suddenly the cabbie let out a gruff mumble. Nicole opened her eyes and sat up. "What?"

The driver muttered again, then gestured out the side window. Nicole blinked, her stomach flip-flopping as she realized that this was going to be a familiar motif for the next few months—her feeling stupid while she hopelessly attempted to understand what someone was saying.

"Excuse me?" she asked weakly. Suddenly remembering one useful French phrase she'd learned long ago from Miss Piggy, she added, "Er, *excus-ay moi*?"

Letting out a loud sigh, the cabbie twisted halfway around to look at her. "La Tour Eiffel," he said. "*Regardez là!* Over there!"

Nicole finally realized what he was trying to tell her. Visible in the distance over the top of some nearby buildings was the tall, sweeping form of the Eiffel Tower. She had seen it many times, of course, in movies or on posters. Seeing it now, through the smudged car window, gave her a strange feeling of disbelief. Was she really here?

She watched the Tower until it slid out of view behind the cab, then closed her eyes again. Why did her parents think seeing a foreign culture was such a great thing, anyway?

At least she was going to be staying with an American family. That was probably the only silver lining in this whole giant storm cloud. The S.A.S.S. program sponsoring her trip counted on local families to help house the students during their stay, and the Smiths—a good, all-American name if Nicole had ever heard one—were one of the host families. Of course, their last name was all she knew about them other than their address, which made her a little nervous.

With my luck, they'll probably be some supersnobby artsy-fartsy types from New York City, Nicole thought, trying to ignore the bumps in the road and sudden turns, which weren't doing anything to improve the state of her stomach. *The kind of people Zara calls PPs—Pretentious Poseurs. They'll dress all in black and insult my haircut and say "Maryland? Isn't that somewhere on Long Island?" Then again, maybe they'll turn out to be Ma and Pa Smith from Yeehaw Station, Texas, with tons of oil money they spend on hairspray and diamond-studded tank tops. They'll call everyone "hon" and pronounce their own name "Smee-ya-uth" and have accents so thick I'll have to ask the Frenchies to translate for me....*

As the car jerked to a stop at the curb, interrupting her anxious fantasies, Nicole opened her eyes and sat up. "Are we here?" she blurted.

The cabbie didn't bother to answer. He just waved a

hand toward a nearby building, then climbed out of the cab to get her luggage.

Nicole rolled down the window all the way and looked outside. They were in the middle of another residential block, this one a little quieter and posher-looking than most of the others they had passed through, with stately shade trees lining the street. The building the driver had indicated was four stories tall, with iron railings along the front steps and in front of each window. A small patch of blooming flowers added a spot of color on either side of the steps. There were no people in sight at the moment.

She sucked in a deep breath but immediately regretted it when, at that very moment, the cabbie leaned down to her window and exhaled, sending a puff of foul gray smoke into the backseat. Nicole coughed as smoke filled her throat, combining with her nervousness to make her suddenly feel sick and shaky all over.

"All right, mademoiselle?" the cabbie asked, his gruff voice for the first time showing a hint of concern. He cast his cigarette down and stepped on it before opening her door.

"Yes, thanks," Nicole choked out, trying to stop her throat from spasming.

She lurched out of the cab, almost tripping over the curb. The world seemed to tip and sway as she took a step forward. Feeling her stomach rolling unpleasantly, she

opened her mouth to take in another deep breath, hoping
to regain control of herself.

But it was too late. Before she could finish inhaling, or
even raise a hand to her mouth, Nicole felt her body involuntarily jerking forward. A split second later she spewed
the contents of her stomach—including those last familiar
bits of American food from the plane—all over the quiet
Parisian sidewalk.

Chapter Two

For a horrifying moment Nicole just stood there, frozen with embarrassment. The cabdriver had jumped back during the actual barfing, but now he stepped forward and patted her tentatively on the back.

"Mademoiselle," he said, not unkindly. "It is okay? You are sick?"

"Sorry," Nicole gasped, wiping her mouth with the back of her hand. "I'm so sorry."

To her complete and utter humiliation, the formerly quiet street suddenly seemed to be turning into Grand Central Station. Or whatever the French equivalent would

be. Out of the corner of her eye, Nicole was aware of several people peering down at her from windows on both sides of the street. Others seemed to be wandering toward her from up and down the block.

The cabdriver patted her on the back again. "I fetch rest of the baggage, yes?" he said helpfully, disappearing back around to the cab's trunk.

As Nicole stood there, breathing hard and wishing she could sink into the sidewalk and disappear, a man and woman emerged from the building and hurried down the steps toward her. Both appeared to be in their fifties or early sixties; the man was slight and not terribly tall, with a full head of graying brown hair and kind eyes. He was wearing a dapper suit with a handkerchief sticking out of the breast pocket. The woman's gray-streaked auburn hair was swept up into an elegant bun, and she was just as stylishly dressed as her companion. Her face, while showing the lines and creases of age, was as beautiful as a marble statue, with high cheekbones, a small but aristocratic nose, and intelligent light blue eyes.

Nicole hardly had time to wonder whether these people could be her host family when they were upon her. "My dear girl," the woman said. "Are you all right? My husband and I were just heading out for a walk when we saw what happened." Her English was flawless but unmistakably French-accented, giving Nicole the answer to her question. Not the Smiths. Just some French people.

"I'm okay." Nicole smiled weakly, feeling self-conscious. The puddle was still right there by her feet, and she was sure her breath couldn't be smelling too good at the moment. "No problem."

The man swept his handkerchief from his pocket and held it out to her. "Here you are, *ma chère*," he said. "You might need this."

"Oh! That's okay." Nicole did her best to wave away his offer. But he pressed the handkerchief into her hand insistently. Feeling foolish, she took it and dabbed at the corners of her mouth.

"That's better." The woman smiled. "Now, let me guess. You must be Nicole."

"The Smiths have been talking about you for weeks," the husband added. "Oh! But how rude of us—we have not introduced ourselves. I'm Renaud Durand, and this is my wife, Marie."

"Nice to meet you," Nicole said automatically. But her attention was no longer on the older couple. Another person was approaching from down the block—a young guy wearing jeans and a curious expression.

Renaud turned away and began speaking rapidly in French to the driver, who had finished unloading Nicole's luggage and was hovering nearby. Marie picked up one of the smaller suitcases and turned toward the steps.

"Stay right here with Renaud a moment and rest," she said. "I shall tell the Smiths you have arrived."

"Oh, you don't have to…." Nicole let her voice trail off, since Marie was already hurrying up the steps without a backward glance.

Meanwhile the blue jean–wearing guy was still heading her way, staring at her with interest. Nicole gulped and tried not to stare back. When he got closer, she could see that he was probably only two or three years older than she was. He was lean and tall, with dark hair that was cut short and spiky. His green eyes sparkled, and his lips were curled into a slight smile. He was probably one of the cutest guys she'd ever seen in person.

"Bonjour," he said to her, followed by a couple more sentences in French.

Trying not to glance down at the puddle, Nicole forced a tight smile. "Hi," she said shortly. "Sorry, I don't speak French." She scanned her mind, trying to recall the phrase her father had taught her. *"Je ne parloy,* um…"

She was irritated to see that the guy's smile had broadened into an amused grin. "It is all right, do not worry, *ça va,"* he said. "I speak English."

"Goody for you," Nicole muttered under her breath. "If you'll excuse me, I have to take care of my bags."

"May I help?" The guy stepped forward immediately, already reaching for the nearest suitcase.

Nicole blocked him by grabbing it herself. "No thanks," she said shortly. "I've got it covered."

"Ah, but it is no trouble," he said. "I think we are going to the same place."

Nicole blinked, trying to figure out what he was talking about. He took advantage of her confusion by grabbing a different bag and taking off with it up the steps of the building Marie had entered.

Trying to figure out if this could possibly be some weird French type of mugging, Nicole took a step after him. Just then, as the taxi peeled off from the curb, Renaud turned toward her. "That is all taken care of," he said with a smile. "Feeling better? Come, let's get your things inside."

Despite Nicole's protests, he insisted on taking the two heaviest suitcases himself, leaving her with just her garment bag, a smaller duffel, and the padded case containing her laptop. She slung the bags over her shoulders and followed Renaud toward the steps. They were halfway up the stairs when the door swung open and a plump, pretty, rosy-cheeked woman of about forty hurried out.

"Nicole!" she exclaimed. "Welcome! I'm Lynn Smith. Are you all right? Marie tells me you're not feeling well."

At the sound of the woman's stout middle-American accent, Nicole felt like crying with relief. "Hi," she said, cracking her first real smile since her plane had left American soil. "Yeah, I guess I got a little carsick on the way over. Sorry about your sidewalk."

Mrs. Smith brushed away her concern. "Don't worry

about that, sweetie. Now come on inside and sit down. I'll fix you some tea while we get to know each other, and we'll have you feeling better in no time."

"Thanks." Nicole allowed herself to be bustled up the steps and through the tall, carved-wood front door of the building.

"There are five apartments in this building," Mrs. Smith explained as she led the way toward a narrow set of stairs at the back of the hall. "Renaud and Marie live there"—she waved a hand toward a door as they passed—"and we've got the whole second floor. Well, they call it the first floor here, I think." She laughed heartily. "I still don't have that one figured out, I'm afraid."

Behind her, Nicole heard Renaud chuckle. She smiled weakly, not really getting the joke.

Soon Mrs. Smith was pushing open a door on the second floor. "Guess who's here?" she sang out.

Her question was met with a sudden howling, shrieking explosion of noise. Nicole barely had time to register her first impression of the Smiths' apartment—comfortable, colorful, and cluttered—before a couple of children, the sources of the noise, hurled themselves toward her.

"Whoa," she said, involuntarily taking a quick step back.

"Kids!" Mrs. Smith said sharply. "Settle."

"That's right," a deep, cheerful male voice put in. A man—Mr. Smith, Nicole assumed—stepped into view from another room, his broad-shouldered bulk and shock of red hair seeming too big and bright for the relatively small room. "At least let her get inside before you attack."

The two young children—a redheaded boy who looked about five or six years old, and a pigtailed blond girl a year or two younger—obediently fell silent.

"This is my husband, Ed," Mrs. Smith said. "He was invited to teach at the Sorbonne for a couple of years, which is why we're all here. And this is Brandon and Marissa," she added, gesturing at the children.

"It's great to have you with us, Nicole." Mr. Smith stepped forward to take her hand in a grip that was as strong and hearty as his booming voice. "Please treat our home as your own. We want you to feel welcome."

Then send me back home, Nicole thought, *because that's the only place I'm ever going to feel really welcome.* But she kept that thought to herself, smiling and mumbling something polite as she shook his hand.

Over at the door Renaud said a quick, polite good-bye and headed downstairs to his own apartment. At about the same time, a thin wail drifted in from an unseen room.

"Oh, dear." Mrs. Smith glanced at her husband. "Sounds like the twins are awake."

"Don't worry, Luc's in there with them," Mr. Smith said.

"Ah, good." Mrs. Smith ushered Nicole farther into the room and sat her down on an overstuffed sofa. Judging by its faded floral fabric and lumpy arms, it clearly had seen better days, but it was surprisingly comfortable. "Luc is our

nanny," she explained. "He's just wonderful with the children—I couldn't survive without him."

"You have a male nanny?" Nicole said in surprise. Her mind flashed to a vision of her cabdriver scowling at a couple of babies and flicking ashes onto them. She had to swallow back a sudden giggle.

"Oh, yes, he's fantastic. He comes four days a week—which lets me have some quiet time to do my writing, and it works out well with his college schedule, too....Oh! Here he is now." She gazed toward the door with a smile. "Luc, come meet Nicole."

Nicole froze. There, staring back at her from the doorway, a baby in each arm, was the cute green-eyed guy from outside.

Before she could figure out how to react, his face broke into an amused grin.

"Oui," he told the Smiths. "We have already met."

From: NicLar@email.com

To: PatriceQT@email.com; ZZZar@email.com; anniegood@email.com

Subject: Ugh!

Hey u guys, I'm here.

:-p

I miss u all already. Do u miss me??? I hope so! bc the

only thing keeping me going is thinking of u guys. AAAAAH! Y did my parents do this 2 me?? it's not like just being in paris is suddenly going 2 make me say, hey! I changed my mind; Ivy League here I come! Duh. Y don't they get that??

Anyway, the Smiths (my host family) r ok, but they have like a million little kids. U know I'm good w/kids, right? But these r NOT normal kids. They don't talk—they YELL! They don't walk—they RUN! Get the pic? Last night at dinner, boykid chewed w/his mouth open the whole time, & no 1 said anything! Gross!

They also have, get this, a male nanny. A manny! His name is Luc and he's this totally snooty French college guy. A total flirt, 2—way 2 stuck on himself, like he thinks I should b totally drooling over him or something. He offered 2 show me around the neighborhood about 50 million times. (Of course I said thnx, but no thnx.) Bright side, at least he's EZ on the eyes…(don't tell N I said that tho!!! haha.)

O well, guess I better get some sleep. My classes start 2morrow and I don't want 2 fall asleep on my 1st day. Or maybe I do… if only I could fall asleep and wake up at the end of the semester…

Luv,
yr depressed friend,
Nic

• • •

"Thanks for the ride," Nicole told Mr. Smith.

"No problem," Mr. Smith replied jovially, shifting his car into neutral. "Figured I could be a little late so I could drop you off—after all, it's probably a bit much for you to tackle the *métro* on your first day."

He laughed heartily at his own comment. Nicole had already figured out that the *métro* was the Parisian subway system, and she really wasn't looking forward to learning anything more about it. She wondered if she could convince Mr. Smith to drive her every day. Saying good-bye, she climbed out of the car and watched it disappear into the passing traffic.

She was standing in front of a large stone building. Flags from at least a dozen nations, including the United States, flew from the roof, and a pair of stone lions flanked the steps leading up to a pair of iron-studded wooden doors. The place looked more like some kind of fortress or museum than a school.

Is this really me standing here? she wondered, focusing on the familiar red, white, and blue pattern of the American flag flapping in the breeze overhead. *Am I about to walk into this building and start school in this foreign place?*

Her mind shied away from the question. More than anything, she wished she could avoid the whole thing;

wake up to the sound of her pink heart-shaped alarm clock beeping out the call to her first day of school back home at Peabody High.

She stared at the rough stone facade of the building, willing her fantasy to come true. But the stones held up to her gaze, solid and gray and unresponsive. Her stomach was jumping around, reminding her of the countless times she'd stood before other unfamiliar school buildings, psyching herself up to go in and face yet another roomful of strangers. She sighed and took a step toward the door, through which people had been pouring the whole time she stood there.

One of them caught her eye. Just a few yards away from where Nicole was standing, a tall, slim, stylishly dressed blond girl was rummaging through her purse. The girl's straight, shoulder-length hair was several shades lighter than Nicole's, her eyes clear sky blue, her skin lightly tanned and flawless. Overall, the blond girl looked as much like a fashion model as anyone Nicole had ever seen.

When the girl turned and met her gaze, Nicole belatedly realized she was staring.

"Hallo." The girl stepped toward Nicole with a tentative but friendly smile. "I am Annike. Are you a new student here as well?"

"Huh? Oh! Yes," Nicole blurted out, caught off guard. "I mean, yeah, I'm Nicole. I'm S.A.S.S.—I mean, I'm here with

the S.A.S.S. program. I'm supposed to start classes here today."

"Oh, good!" Annike's smile brightened, making her look more beautiful than ever. She had a strong accent, though it didn't sound French. "I am S.A.S.S., too. I am so nervous that I am a little frightened to go inside by myself."

"Me, too." Nicole was relieved to hear someone else admit something like that. Especially someone as poised as this girl. "I still can't believe I'm here, you know? I mean, I don't even speak French or anything. Oh, I'm American, by the way, in case you couldn't tell."

"You don't say?" Annike winked. "I'm from Sweden. Stockholm. I've only ever been to Paris a handful of times before on holiday—it's all so new to be living here. But I do have a little French, at least. Maybe I can help you learn, if you like?"

"Thanks." Nicole wasn't sure she would be taking Annike up on that offer anytime soon. She might have to suffer through language class, but that didn't mean she actually had to learn the language. That would be like admitting she didn't mind being here. "Um, I guess we'd better get inside or we'll be late."

As they headed up the stairs, the two girls chatted about their schedules. Nicole discovered that Annike was in her culinary-arts class. Nicole had signed up for the elective mostly to spite her parents, who would have preferred she choose one of the more mind-expanding offerings such as Worlds of Philosophy or International Theories of Basket Weaving.

"Oh, I cannot wait," Annike said enthusiastically as they discussed the culinary-arts course. "I simply adore French food, don't you?"

Nicole smiled weakly, realizing she hadn't really stopped to consider all the implications of taking a cooking class in a foreign land. Oops.

"I am also taking Paris Through an Artist's Eye," Annike added. "That one should be fantastic! I talked to someone who took it last term, and he said it was the best. They got to go to a really good play, and visited a big fashion show."

"Huh?" Despite Annike's almost perfect English, Nicole wondered if they were having translation problems. "Wait, I'm taking that one, too. But I thought it was, like, an art-appreciation class or something."

"Oh, yes," Annike assured her. "But it is much better than that—I think more of a culture-appreciation class. We will cover architecture, and literature, and music, and film, and philosophy, and ways of seeing..."

Nicole tuned out. The more Annike went on about the course, the more Nicole's heart sank. She'd expected a dull hour spent napping through poorly lit slide shows or trudging through dusty museums staring at boring paintings of fruit baskets and landscapes. That she would have

been able to handle. This? She wasn't so sure.

The interior of the school building turned out to be just as gray and forbidding as the exterior. Stopping in the crowded lobby, Annike turned and smiled rather anxiously at Nicole.

"I wish we had one of our classes together right away," she said. "I'm so nervous! I've never been to a school where I didn't know anyone."

"I have," Nicole admitted. "Unfortunately. See, my parents are landscapers—they create gardens for people. Big ones, I mean, like new parks and giant estates and stuff, you know?"

"Oh, what a cool job!" Annike exclaimed, her eyes widening. "It must be such fun to observe their work, no?"

Nicole had never really thought of it that way. "I guess," she said. "But it really stunk for me growing up, since we had to move pretty much every time they finished a job and went on to a new one."

Annike nodded sympathetically. "Ach, I would think so," she murmured. "An adventure for them but just a big change for you..."

Nicole didn't usually spill her guts to people she'd just met. But Annike seemed so sympathetic that it didn't even feel weird.

Just then a very tall, very thin girl rushed past them so fast that her elbow hit Nicole's backpack, sending it flying.

It crashed to the floor at Annike's feet, spilling notebooks and pens everywhere.

"Oh, so sorry!" the tall girl cried in an Australian accent, stopping and turning back to help. "I'm such a drongo today...."

"That's okay." Nicole crouched down to gather her things. "No biggie."

Annike and the other girl both bent to help. "My name's Ada," the tall girl said. "Are you lot here for the S.A.S.S. program, too?" Without giving either of them a chance to respond, she went on, "Jingoes, but I'm nervous about today! I'm supposed to be in Euro-history class right now, and the room number is all smudged on my form, so I have no idea where to go."

"European history?" Nicole glanced up. "Is your teacher Mr. Jenks? I have that one now, too. And yeah, we're both with S.A.S.S., too." She gestured toward Annike.

"Brilliant!" Ada smiled with relief at both of them before focusing again on Nicole. "Mind if I tag along with you to history, then? I swear I won't knock you over again. At least I'll try not to."

Nicole giggled. "Sounds like a plan. I'm Nicole, by the way."

Somehow, just meeting a couple of her fellow students was making her feel a little less anxious about things. Annike and Ada both seemed really nice.

"Bye, then," Annike said, sounding a little sad. "I've got my French-language class now. But I'll see you two later, okay?"

"Okay." Nicole smiled and waved as the other girl hurried off. Then she turned toward Ada. "Ready?"

"I'm as ready as I'll ever be," Ada declared with a mock shiver.

Yeah, Nicole thought as the two of them headed off down the hall. *I second that.*

Chapter Three

From: ZZZar@email.com
To: NicLar@email.com
Subject: re: Ugh!

Yo babe! Wearing a beret yet? j/k—you and I both know hats are not yr friend. Heh.

So things here r cool. Got Mopey Miller for precalc, and you know what that means—yearlong par-tay! Heh. A and P are both in my class, too.

On the Hottie Horizon, cute new guy in my English class. Def DTHB material. Will b moving in 4 the kill b4 long.

Have some extra stinky cheese for me (not),

Z

"*Bonjour,* students. Welcome to Introductory French."

Nicole forced a smile as her French-language teacher, a beaming young man with a prominent Adam's apple, looked around the classroom. The class was her second to last of the day, and she was already counting the seconds until she could escape.

It's only my first day, and I'm sick of this whole deal already, Nicole thought. *How am I going to survive three months of this?*

Just then the door burst open and Ada rushed in. "Sorry!" she cried, red-faced and flustered. "I mean, er, *pardon*? Um, is this my French class?"

A few of the other students tittered. Nicole winced on Ada's behalf, though the Australian girl didn't really look that embarrassed.

The teacher smiled. "Let me guess," he said in heavily accented English. "You are Mademoiselle Ada Williamson, *n'est-ce pas*?"

"Too right—uh, I mean *oui*, that's me," Ada replied cheerfully. "So I am in the right place!"

"Please take a seat, mademoiselle," the teacher said, looking amused. "We were just about to get started."

Ada glanced around the room. When she spotted Nicole, her face lit up. "G'day, Nicole," she said, taking the empty seat beside her. "It's nice to see a friendly face."

"Ditto," Nicole replied, feeling a little better herself. She'd had the same feeling earlier that day after walking into her French cooking class and seeing Annike smiling at her. "So how have you been making out since history class?" she asked Ada.

"Doing all right," Ada replied. "Other than being late for nearly every class—I just can't seem to find my way around this place. My teachers must think I'm a total yobbo!" She laughed, seeming amused at her own ineptitude. "Oh hey, where did you wind up for lunch? I looked for you outside, but I wasn't sure if we had the same break—I've got second-hour lunch."

"Me, too." Nicole was touched that the other girl had looked for her. If only she'd known that, maybe she wouldn't have spent her lunch hour sitting by herself at Mickey D's.

Just then the teacher called for attention. At least that's what Nicole guessed he was doing, since he did it in French. He then launched into a speech about the goals of the class and the history of the French language. Thankfully, that part was in English.

"All right, class," he added at last. "Now I think we will

begin with a class exercise, a way to get to know one another, eh? I want you to look at this list of basic French words and phrases and try to use some of them in a conversation with your neighbor. I will move around helping with your pronunciation."

Ada turned to Nicole as the teacher started passing out the papers. "Partners?"

"Absolutely," Nicole replied. "Um, do you speak any French at all?"

"Not worth a zack," Ada replied with a laugh. Seeing Nicole's confused expression, she added, "I mean, not at all. What about you?"

Nicole shook her head. "Nope. I take Spanish back home. So I'm pretty much clueless." She sighed. "And not just about the language, either..." she added under her breath.

Ada shot her a sympathetic look. "No worries, Nic," she said. "I'm sure it will all get easier—you'll see."

To Nicole's surprise, Ada was right. It did get easier—at least a little. With each passing day of her first week she was able to find her way around a little more smoothly. By Thursday, when she arrived at French cooking class, her daily schedule was starting to feel familiar, if not yet totally comfortable.

Annike was waiting at their workstation. The classroom consisted of a dozen large, marble topped cooking stations. Though each station included a stainless-steel stove and sink, Nicole suspected the room had been remodeled out of an old science lab. Whenever the stoves heated up, the whole place smelled faintly of formaldehyde.

"Bonjour," Annike greeted her. Then she nodded toward Nicole's feet. "Oh, good. You remembered to wear comfortable shoes."

Nicole glanced down at her sneakers. "Huh?" she said, wondering if Annike's comment had lost something in translation.

"Did you forget? Today is our first field trip in Eye!" That was their shorthand for Paris Through an Artist's Eye, the art and culture class that they shared with Ada.

"Whoops. I guess I did forget." Now that Annike had reminded her, Nicole vaguely recalled their teacher mentioning the trip. The teacher had also mentioned that the reason the Artist's Eye class always fell at the end of the day was to allow more time for frequent field trips around the city—just one more thing Nicole hadn't realized when she'd signed up for the class.

For some reason, Annike seemed excited at the prospect of their extended school day. "I can't wait—I adore the Louvre!" she exclaimed.

"That's, like, a big famous art museum, right?" Nicole did her best to seem interested. She'd pretty much zoned out while their teacher had described the trip, finding her own doodle of Nate's name much more fascinating than

listening to the details of some deadly-dull museum.

"Yes—the biggest and famous-est. You'll love it!"

"Maybe." This time Nicole couldn't help sounding dubious. "Museums aren't really my thing, though."

"Really? Well, perhaps the Louvre will help to change your mind about that."

Just then their cooking teacher called the class to attention. Nicole slumped on her stool, feeling unsettled.

Okay, it's nice that I'm making some friends here, sort of, she thought with a sidelong glance at Annike. *But in a way, hanging out with Annike and Ada is making me miss my real friends even more—friends who like the same things I like. I mean, how weird is it for someone my age to actually be psyched about going to some stuffy art museum?*

She shook her head as the teacher continued with her directions. Was she ever going to feel like she really fit in here? And more importantly—did she even want to?

"...and here we have a piece known as *Moroccan Notebook* by Eugène Delacroix. In the year 1832 the artist brought this notebook with him to Tangiers, and we can see before us a blend of notes and sketches, which..."

Nicole's mind wandered as the Louvre museum guide, a short French man, droned on and on about the piece in front of the group. Nicole wasn't sure why he was spending so much time on it; it looked like nothing more than a bunch of scribbles on old yellowed paper. She glanced around and found that no one else looked as bored as she felt. The rest of the Artist's Eye class was listening politely. Even Finn and Seamus, the pair of lively Irish friends she'd already secretly nicknamed the wonder twins—as in, she wondered if they ever stopped talking, moving, kidding around, shoving at each other—seemed to be paying attention. Annike and Ada were also gazing raptly at the piece as if it held the meaning of life.

She sighed. While she had to admit that some things about the Louvre were kind of cool, such as seeing the *Mona Lisa* and other famous paintings, she was already getting a little bored. Plus her feet were starting to hurt. Whatever else the Louvre might be, it was definitely *big*.

The course teacher, Dr. Morley, stepped forward and took over the lecture from the boring guide. "Thank you, monsieur," she said to him in her crisp British accent. "Very interesting."

Nicole snapped back to attention. Dr. Morley had that effect on people. Almost six feet tall, with flaming red hair, a large beaklike nose, and a penchant for flowing dresses, Elizabeth Morley was practically a force of nature. Her unusual appearance was topped only by her vibrant personality. She was the type of person who might do or say something outrageous at any moment, which made Nicole a little nervous.

"Now then, class," the teacher said. "Who can say how

this piece is filtered through the lens of Romanticism, as we discussed yesterday?"

Nicole shrank back, trying to avoid her teacher's quick, roving eye. She had barely paid attention to the previous day's lecture on different art styles, and couldn't recall just what was so unique about Romanticism. Somehow she knew it probably didn't have anything in common with the pink-and-red Valentine's Day card Nate had given her last year.... Luckily at least half of her dozen classmates were already raising their hands, eager to answer the question.

Dr. Morley pointed to one of them, a petite, bright-eyed Australian girl named Janet. "Yes?" the teacher said. "Let's hear it, then."

"Well, first of all, Delacroix definitely used, you know, bold and dramatic lines and stuff," Janet began with obvious enthusiasm. "And also it's an exotic setting, as you were saying they liked, and..."

Nicole zoned out again as Janet babbled fervently about emotion and nostalgia and all sorts of other things that didn't seem to have much to do with the rough little drawings of people and mountains and windows in front of them. *I should be at home dozing through precalculus class with my friends right now,* Nicole thought, *then gossiping about the new cute boys in school and beginning the quest for the perfect homecoming dress. But no, instead I'm here in a foreign country with a bunch of art freaks.*

It seemed like forever before the others finally stopped gushing over the sketches and trooped off toward the next room. Nicole trailed along at the back of the group, wishing she could duck out to the gift shop or cafeteria or something.

"Having a nice time?" Annike fell into step beside her. "This is great, isn't it? I mean, I have visited the Louvre before, of course, but I never have seen it like this…."

Nicole forced a smile. "Yeah," she said. "It's great. Um, so you're pretty into art and stuff, huh?"

"Only to look at." Annike laughed. "I cannot draw at all—not even a stick person. What about you? You seem creative—do you paint or anything?"

"Um, not really."

Just then the museum guide started speaking again, and Annike shot Nicole a quick smile before pushing forward for a better view of the next piece. Nicole stayed where she was, a little surprised by Annike's comment.

Creative? Me? Nicole thought. *I wonder where she got that from….*

Nicole's eyes stayed on Annike. How did she do it? She seemed so calmly self-confident, so genuinely pleased to be wherever she was at the time. It reminded Nicole of Zara; one of the things she'd always admired about her friend was the way she seemed to be in command of every situation. Nicole couldn't help envying people like that. Why couldn't she be a little more like them?

Nicole Larson: Class journal

We went to the Louvre today. Seeing the Mona Lisa in person was sort of interesting, even though it was smaller than I expected. Still, I can tell my kids someday that I was there and saw it for real. I guess that's pretty cool. Oh, and they also had the original painting of that poster Dad bought me when he came here years ago for a botany conference or something—turns out it's called The Ray of Sunlight *and it's by some Dutch painter, I forget who. We saw a bunch of other kinds of art, too, like Egyptian antiquities and lots of naked sculptures and some really weird furniture and stuff. I didn't realize the Louvre had more than just paintings, but it turns out they do.*

"So what are you doing this weekend, Nicole?"

Nicole glanced up from packing her books into her backpack. Annike was smiling down at her, looking way too fresh-faced and beautiful for the wrong end of a full day of classes. It was Friday, and their Artist's Eye class had spent almost the whole hour talking about the trip to the Louvre the day before, which had made Nicole a little sleepy. Most of the other students were still hanging around in little groups near the front of the room continu-

40

ing the discussion, while Ada was in the midst of an animated conversation with Dr. Morley herself.

"I—I'm not sure yet." Nicole suddenly felt anxious. Someone like Annike was probably full of fabulous plans— going to clubs, shopping for haute couture on the Champs-Élysées—and Nicole didn't want to admit that she hadn't even thought about how she was going to fill her first weekend in Paris. "I think my host family probably has a few things planned or something," she added weakly.

"Sounds lovely. Enjoy!" Annike gave her a friendly wave, slung her stylish leather bag over one shoulder, and hurried out of the room.

Nicole sighed, feeling like the world's biggest loser. If she were back home where she belonged, she would have had a good answer to Annike's question. She would be looking forward to a full schedule for the weekend—Friday night at a house party with Nate and their friends, Saturday at the mall or the flea market or playing tennis with Zara. Then came Saturday night—date night—when Nate would appear at her door smelling of sandalwood and looking so cute she could hardly stand it, after which he would whisk her off to Lucky Chin's for Chinese food or perhaps Luigi's for the Italian buffet, followed by a drive to their favorite make-out spot. Sunday she would go over to Annie's house for bagels as usual and tell her girlfriends all about her date, then listen as Zara and Annie described their own evenings with the latest in their long line of guys

and Patrice bemoaned another Saturday night spent watching TV with her boyfriend Hank.

Thinking about that made Nicole's heart ache like crazy. Trying to take her mind off it, she quickly gathered up her things and scurried out of the room before any of her other classmates tried to talk to her. At the moment she wasn't sure she could respond without bursting into tears.

She felt a little better once she was out in the fresh, warm, late-afternoon air. Taking a few deep breaths to steady her nerves, she shifted her backpack to the other shoulder so she could reach her purse.

She dug into her change pouch, which felt alarmingly light. When she opened her wallet and flipped through the Monopoly-money–looking euro bills, she found that there weren't many left. She was going through her spending money fast, mostly by taking taxis back and forth to school every day. If she didn't cool it, she wasn't going to have enough to buy lunch next week.

But she was ready to forget about that, at least for one more day. It was Friday—she wasn't in the mood to figure out the *métro* on the last day of a tough week. She would just take one more cab, maybe pack a lunch a couple of days next week to make up for it....Then she remembered that she'd been planning a nice, leisurely long-distance call with Nate over the weekend. It was just about the only thing keeping her sane, and she didn't want to risk having to cut it short. That meant she needed to save a decent chunk of cash so she could either buy a phone card or pay the Smiths for the international call.

That settled it. She was going to have to try to figure out the *métro*. Now.

Descending into the station felt like descending into hell. It was warm outside, but the air in the tunnel was hot, damp, and sticky, as if millions of unseen people were breathing out at her all the time. Nicole felt her hair go limp and her upper lip bead with sweat.

"I can't believe the D.C. metro is actually named for *this*," she murmured under her breath as she took in the station, which seemed to be coated with a layer of dust and grunge that hadn't been touched since the French Revolution. It was nothing like the airy, whitewashed look of the metro stations in Washington D.C. It reminded her more of the subway her family had taken from the train station to their hotel on her one and only trip to New York City. Except that here, all the graffiti was written in French.

Earlier in the week the Smiths had carefully explained how the *métro* worked. Aside from the name of their stop, Nicole didn't remember any of it now. Spotting a map on the wall, she walked over and scanned the jumble of red, black, yellow, and green lines with their foreign-sounding labels, desperately waiting for something on it to look familiar.

By some miracle, she finally spotted the name of the Smiths' stop. She found her way to what she hoped was

the right section of track just as a train clattered into the station and its doors opened with a whoosh.

"Excuse me!" she blurted as someone bumped into her, almost sending her into the side of the train. Catching her balance, she hung back, waiting for a break in the flow of people rushing in and out of the car.

Finally realizing that break might never come, she took a deep breath and plunged forward. Seconds later she found herself standing inside the subway car.

The doors slid shut, and the train lurched into motion. Nicole grabbed at a pole and glanced around. The *métro* car was crowded, but there were several seats free. Letting go of the pole, she collapsed into the closest one.

The *métro* car swayed as it shuddered to a stop at the next station, and Nicole clutched at the armrest of her seat. She glanced out the grimy window beside her. There were so many people waiting on the platform outside that for a moment she couldn't see anything else, including the sign identifying the station.

When she did, she frowned. The name didn't seem quite right.

Before she could decide what to do, the doors slid shut again and the train moved on. *Oh well*, she thought. *I'm sure it's fine. I just have to Zen out, like Zara always says, and stop giving myself an ulcer. I'll get there when I get there. Maybe...*

For the next few minutes she comforted herself by

watching people get on and off the train. Now and then she glanced nervously out the window, a little afraid to pay too much attention to the signs flashing past. She still had the uneasy feeling she might have picked the wrong train. After all, what did she know about public transportation? On the rare occasions when she went into Washington or Baltimore, she counted on either her parents, Zara, or Nate to take care of the details.

As the train wheezed out of yet another unfamiliar-sounding stop, Nicole finally decided she had to risk speaking to one of the other passengers. Otherwise she might end up out in the French countryside somewhere.

It took only two tries to find someone who spoke English. When Nicole mentioned where she was trying to go, a little old lady in a lacy black shawl shook her head sadly.

"Ah, *chérie*," she said. "You are going the wrong way. Here is what you must do—get off at the next station, and then…"

Nicole couldn't quite follow the torrent of directions the old lady added after that. She was too busy trying to keep her tears from spilling over. If she started crying now, she was afraid she might not be able to stop.

"Th-thank you," she managed to croak out just as the subway car shuddered to a stop at the next station.

Standing up, she allowed the other disembarking passengers to sweep her out the door and up the stairs. Then

she stopped, looking around anxiously. There was another *métro* map here, but the very thought of trying to decipher it brought her to the verge of tears again. Her next thought was to go out and hail a taxi, but for all she knew, she might be miles from home, which would mean the fare could eat up the rest of her money.

Instead, she found a pay phone near the station doors. Feeling very glad that numbers were the same in every language, she punched in the Smiths' number.

To her relief, she heard Mrs. Smith's cheery voice at the other end of the line. She wasn't sure she could have spoken if Luc had been the one to answer.

"Hello?" Nicole's voice cracked. A wave of shame swept over her. "Um, it's Nicole. I think I really messed up...."

Chapter Four

From: NicLar@email.com
To: N8THEGR8@email.com
Subject: Miss ya!

Hey Sweetie,

It's me again! I can't wait 2 hear yr voice—I know it's only been a week, but it feels more like a million yrs!!! Thinking about talking 2 u is the only thing that kept me going the last few days...

Anyway, since I know u get up 2morrow at 7 am 4 foot-

ball practice, I'm going 2 try 2 call u then. I can't wait any
l8r than that! So make sure u keep ur cell turned on, OK?

Love u 4ever,
Nic

From: N8THEGR8@email.com
To: NicLar@email.com
Subject: re: Miss ya!

Hi back! Or should I say, bonjurno or whatever?
So howz everything there? Here stuff is good. Just got
home from a party at Mac's house. Fun, but it wasn't the
same w/o ya!
So now I gotta grab a few hours of zzz's so I won't b
dead at practice 2morro. I'm sure hearing from u will help
wake me up tho...

Till then,
N

"No, no!" With difficulty, Nicole swallowed back her frustra-
tion. Peeling the old-fashioned wooden top out of Brandon's
sticky fingers, she spun it on the living room's wooden
floorboards. "Like this—see? You have to do it quick or it'll
fall over."

"Let me try!" Marissa grabbed the top. "I know how to do it!"

There was an amused chuckle from the direction of the sofa, where Luc was sprawled out reading a book. "Better to listen to her, children," he said. "You are American, so you must do it the American way."

Nicole shot him an irritated glance. "It's not the American way," she said, raising her voice to be heard over the two kids, who were now bickering in French. "It's the *right* way."

He dropped the book on his lap and held up both hands in a gesture of surrender. "*Bien sûr*; you are right. Please forgive me. Perhaps I could apologize further by treating you to dinner? *Êtes-vous libre ce soir?* Are you free this evening?"

Nicole sighed. It was Saturday morning, and she was already in a bad mood. She'd been dying to call Nate since the second she'd awakened that day, but due to the time difference between Paris and Maryland, she had to wait until lunchtime. The hours between now and then were crawling past as slowly as a drunken snail, and nothing she did seemed to speed it up. She'd already done all of her homework, and now she was just looking for something else to distract her. She'd figured that the Smith children might do the trick, but so far their frequent shrieking was just aggravating her all the more.

And then there was Luc. All week long he'd been making

it pretty clear that he thought she was cute. There were the long, lingering looks he gave her every chance he got. The close encounters in the apartment's narrow hallways when their arms or shoulders brushed against each other, just a little. Even the way he said her name—*Neee-cole*—with that slow, slightly crooked smile of his.

It was a bit unsettling to have a gorgeous guy flirting outrageously with her every time they passed each other in the kitchen or outside her room. It wasn't that Nicole didn't have any experience with guys being too forward; on the contrary, before she'd hooked up with Nate she'd had to fight off quite a few pushy guys. But that was different. With American guys there was always an undercurrent of face-saving banter beneath their propositions, which meant all she had to do was come up with a witty response and they would laugh and back down. With Luc, it was hard to tell just how serious he was, and that left her feeling off balance whenever she was around him. Besides, no matter how many times she mentioned Nate's name—or just came right out and reminded Luc that she had a boyfriend back home—he just kept grinning his impossibly handsome grin and trying again.

"Don't listen to anything Nicole says!" Marissa shrieked at her brother with a giggle. "She can't even figure out where to go on the *métro*, remember?"

Nicole gritted her teeth. She'd spent the last eighteen hours trying to forget that little disaster. In response to her frantic phone call, Mrs. Smith had packed all four kids in the car and picked her up at the *métro* station, which turned out to be halfway across the city. Totally embarrassing.

"What was that, Mari?" Luc asked with a sharp flash of interest. "*Répète, s'il te plaît*—what did you say about Nicole and the *métro*?"

"Never mind," Nicole said quickly. "Hey Marissa, want a cookie?"

The little girl ignored the bribe. "Mommy had to go pick her up," she announced. "She was at the wrong station—way far away."

Luc grinned. "Ah, do not tease her, little ones," he chided the children playfully. "One does not need to be clever when one is as beautiful as Mademoiselle Nicole."

That was the last straw.

"Later, kids. I'm going to go for a walk until it's time to call Nate." Without sparing a glance for Luc, she swept from the room with the few shreds of dignity she could muster.

She stomped along for at least six or eight blocks before starting to calm down. Then she slowed her pace and looked around. She had left the residential area behind and reached a busy shopping street packed with strolling Parisians and weekend shoppers. The sound of voices conversing in French drifted toward her from every direction,

annoying her anew. Clenching her fists at her sides, Nicole wondered if it had been a mistake to leave the apartment. After all, wasn't Paris the root of her problem, the very thing she was trying to forget?

Still, she kept walking, hoping the exercise would help clear her head. The last thing she wanted was to be grumpy when it was finally time to call Nate. The two of them would need to pack a week's worth of their relationship into one conversation. It wasn't going to be easy, especially since Nate wasn't all that fond of talking on the phone.

As she walked, Nicole couldn't help noticing that the temperature was almost perfect. It was sunny and warm, but there was none of the oppressive humidity that still lingered back in Maryland at that time of year. Little by little she began to notice other things. The air on this block smelled faintly of baking bread and auto exhaust, a surprisingly pleasant combination. All the buildings seemed to have flowers blooming on the stoops or at the windows. Faint strains of classical music drifted out of the doorway of a restaurant she was passing, along with a tantalizing whiff of melting cheese.

Slowly Nicole felt herself relax. Her steps slowed to a comfortable stroll and her hands unclenched.

Okay, maybe it *was* a good idea to go for a walk. This was kind of almost nice.

She took in the people strolling past, the chatter of voices, the busy storefronts. It was surprising how many French words she already recognized after just a week in her language course. Maybe, just maybe, she could survive this semester after all. Not that she would ever admit that to her parents, of course.

Feeling bold, she decided to step into a bookstore. There were some English-language fashion magazines in the window; she could pick up a few to keep her occupied when she wasn't in class or writing to Nate.

She entered the shop, setting a little bell over the door jingling with silvery tones. The shop was small and seemed dusty, dark, and still after the bright bustle of the street outside. There was no one at the counter, but she soon spotted a battered magazine rack halfway along one wall. She browsed through its contents for a few minutes, impressed by the wide selection. The rack held magazines written in every language she knew of and a few she didn't. She picked out a couple of English-language fashion magazines and headed back toward the front of the shop.

By that time the shopkeeper had appeared behind the sales counter. He was a short, stocky man with a heavy five-o'clock shadow and a rather sour expression. He stared at her fixedly as she approached, neither speaking nor cracking a smile.

Nicole set the magazine on the counter along with a handful of Euros. "Er, *pardon, monsieur?*" She struggled to recall some of the simple phrases she'd learned so far,

though it was hard to keep it from getting mixed up in her mind with her high-school Spanish. "Um...*Je voudrais esto libro*—er, I mean, um..." For the life of her, she couldn't seem to remember the French word for "magazine," or even "book." "Sorry," she added, feeling her face start to go red. "Er, do you speak English? *Parlez-vous—*"

The shopkeeper, who hadn't said a word thus far, suddenly let loose with a barrage of French, speaking so quickly that Nicole couldn't make out a single word. He glowered at her as he spoke, seeming to be insulted by her very existence.

"I—I don't really...Please," Nicole stammered. "I don't understand—*je ne comprendo...*"

She felt flustered, suddenly on the verge of tears. It didn't help that she could hear Zara's sarcastic voice in her head, clear as day—*Gee, what a surprise, a rude person in France.* Wondering if she'd miscalculated the euros—it certainly wouldn't be the first time that had happened—Nicole tried to add a few coins to the pile and wound up dropping them all over the floor. That only seemed to add to the shopkeeper's ire, and his eyes flashed as he growled at her again in French.

Just as Nicole was ready to turn and race out of the shop, leaving both magazine and euros behind, she heard a female voice speak up calmly in French, followed by English: "Is there a problem here, Nicole?"

The shopkeeper shifted his glare from Nicole to the

newcomer, and when Nicole glanced over her shoulder, she saw that the Smiths' downstairs neighbor, Marie Durand, had just entered the shop.

The shopkeeper retorted to Marie's question in French, gesturing curtly toward Nicole. Marie responded to him calmly, her voice crisp and businesslike. Stepping past Nicole, she quickly scooped up about half of the euros Nicole had set down, then pushed the remainder across the counter at the man. Picking up the magazines, she added a few stern words in French. It didn't require being bilingual to understand her point; the shopkeeper glowered, but fell silent and even muttered something in Nicole's general direction that might have been an apology, though Nicole didn't dare respond for fear of setting him off again.

"Come along, Nicole," Marie said serenely. "I think we're finished here."

Numbly, Nicole turned and followed Marie out of the shop. All her feelings of confusion, homesickness, and helplessness welled up, so fast she couldn't stomp them down. Glancing over her shoulder at the bookstore, she burst out without thinking, *"I hate Paris!"*

She realized almost immediately that it hadn't been the most tactful thing to say at the moment. But when she shot Marie a sidelong glance, the older woman didn't seem the least bit insulted or even surprised.

"Come, *chérie*," she suggested as if Nicole hadn't said a word. "Let's go have a drop of tea."

• • •

Fifteen minutes later Nicole was settled in Marie's comfortable, antique-filled parlor holding a fragrant cup of herbal tea on one knee. She had done her best to demur when Marie invited her in, but Marie had been politely insistent, claiming that she needed company since Renaud was away on a weekend trip to visit family. Besides, there was still over an hour before Nicole could try to reach Nate, and she figured almost anything would be better than going back and facing Luc and the kids.

"Now then, Nicole." Marie settled herself with her own cup of tea on a damask-upholstered sofa across from her guest. "Feeling a little better?"

"Sure." Now that the crisis had passed, Nicole was already feeling sheepish about the whole thing. "I guess I just panicked when that guy started yelling."

Marie shook her head and made a soft tut-tut sound. "That man, he is always a—hmm, how would one say it in English? A grump?" She shrugged gracefully. "He fancies himself a bit of a revolutionary, but really he is merely a bully."

Nicole couldn't help smiling at Marie's description. "Really?" she said. "You actually know him, then?"

"Oh, yes. I've lived in this neighborhood for many years. I know almost everyone, I'm afraid." Marie laughed and stirred her tea. "That's the trouble with staying in one place for so long."

Nicole shrugged, thinking of Peabody Corner. "I don't know," she said. "I think it's kind of nice."

"Well, perhaps you are right." Marie smiled. "I think you might be thinking of your own home, no? I would love to hear more about it if you wish to share it."

Nicole didn't need to be asked twice. Aside from a few polite questions from the Smiths, nobody seemed to have any interest at all in hearing about Nicole's hometown or anything else about her real life. "Sure!" she said eagerly. "My town is called Peabody Corner, and I've lived there for almost four years. I have three best friends—girlfriends, I mean. Then there's my boyfriend Nate...."

By the time she headed back upstairs an hour later, Nicole was feeling much better. After talking about herself for a while, she'd started to feel guilty about hogging the limelight and politely asked Marie to tell her more about herself. Marie responded with several surprisingly entertaining stories about her own childhood in several small villages in France and Switzerland. Nicole had shared some of her own feelings about moving around so much in her younger days, and eventually left the first-floor apartment feeling not only that she knew the older woman a little better, but that she truly liked her.

Reaching the second floor, Nicole took a deep breath and tried to prepare herself to face Luc and the Smith kids again. Thanks to Marie's soothing presence, she was pretty

sure she could keep her cool this time. It was nice to know that there was one other sane, normal person around— even if she *was* French.

Smiling at the thought, she opened the door and stepped inside.

"Bonjour," Luc greeted her when she entered the living room. He was sitting on the sofa with a thick textbook while Brandon and Marissa played on the floor nearby. "Back so soon? We missed you, didn't we, little ones?"

"No," Brandon announced, barely glancing up from his blocks.

Marissa glanced at Luc before answering. "Yes!" she cried loudly. "We missed her beauty and...um...What was it again?"

"Her charm," Luc prompted in a loud stage whisper.

"And her charm." Marissa grinned, seeming pleased with herself. "Her charming charm."

Nicole blushed. So now Luc was enlisting the kids to help him hit on her? Great.

"Excuse me. I have a phone call to make," she muttered, stepping toward her room.

But when she checked her watch, she saw that it was still a little early in Maryland. The last thing she wanted to do was wake up Nate before his alarm, especially if he'd been out partying with his friends the night before.

She veered off into the kitchen, which was separated from the living room by a long countertop. Opening the refrigerator door, she grabbed a carton of juice.

"What's she doing?" she heard Brandon say from the other room. "The phone's not in the refrigerator."

"I think she is cooling herself off," Luc replied. His voice was loud enough to carry easily into the kitchen. "Perhaps she is not used to being around such attractive young men as us?"

As Brandon burst into giggles, Nicole rolled her eyes. Typical. Why did Luc insist on being so obnoxious? He knew she had a boyfriend back home.

She grabbed the cordless phone from the counter and escaped to her room. Once inside with the door shut and locked, she sat on the edge of her bed and sipped at her juice, willing the clock to move forward. Finally, as she drained the last sip of her drink, she decided it was late enough. Her heart was pounding with excitement as she carefully dialed the phone number.

It seemed to take forever for the line to connect. Finally she heard ringing on the other end. Pressing the phone to her ear, she held her breath and waited for Nate to pick up.

And waited. And waited some more.

Finally there was a click. Her heart jumped, then sank again as she heard the familiar sound of Nate's voice-mail message: "Yo, this is Nate. You know how this works, so go for it." *Beep!*

Chapter Five

From: PatriceQT@email.com
To: NicLar@email.com
Subject: Life & stuff

Hi Nic,

Sorry to hear u had so much trouble reaching Nate the other day. I'm sure he just spaced on the time—u know how he is. At least u finally got him on the phone in the end? He said u guys didn't get 2 talk 4 very long, but I guess every little bit counts, right?

So how'r things going there? Here it's sameold, same-old. Hank got in trouble w/his coach for being late 2 practice, but then he scored 2 touchdowns in the game last weekend so he's ok now. Nate did really great in the game, 2—no TDs this time, but lots of other good stuff. At the party that night he went nutz & jumped into Janni Trover's pool in nuthin but his boxers. It was only like 50 degrees out that night, too… brr! Good thing coach didn't hear about that, huh?

More later; gotta go help A w/her bio homework.

Love,

P

"All right, people." Dr. Morley glanced down at the silver-filigree pocket watch she always wore on a long chain around her neck. "That just about does it for today's hour. I hope everyone is nearly finished with their class journal entries about our trip to the Louvre because our next field trip will be in three days' time."

"Where are we going?" Seamus called out.

Dr. Morley pursed her lips playfully. "As they say here in France, *tout vient à point pour qui sait attendre*. You will have to wait and see."

The students filed out of the room, most of them buzzing curiously about the upcoming trip. Annike waited for Nicole, and they stepped out into the hall together.

"I wonder where we're going on the field trip." Annike shot a glance back over her shoulder at Dr. Morley, who was standing just inside the classroom door chatting with a couple of their classmates.

Nicole shrugged, not nearly as interested as the rest of the class appeared to be. "Dunno," she said. "Hey, what about what she just said? Did you do your journal entry yet?"

"Of course." Annike seemed slightly surprised by the question. "It's been over a week since we visited the Louvre." She smiled at Nicole. "I wanted to write everything down right off so I wouldn't forget."

Nicole smiled back weakly. It was hard to believe another whole week had passed—each individual hour of each individual day seemed to creep by like molasses. The only time she felt normal was when she was writing e-mails or letters to Nate and her other friends. At school Nicole still felt like an outsider, even though she was becoming pretty good friends with Annike, Ada, and Janet from her Artist's Eye class—pretending to fit in was one of the talents she'd developed growing up.

But she still felt a little tentative about it all. Under other circumstances, she suspected she and Annike, for instance, might become true friends. It was tempting to try to spend more time with her—maybe ask her to hang out on the weekends or something. But was it worth the effort? After all, in a few months Nicole would be heading back to Maryland and would probably never see any of her Paris schoolmates again. Why waste the energy getting to know them any better when, at best, she might end up with a pen pal at the end of the semester?

As the two girls stepped out through the school doors into the bright afternoon sunshine, Annike turned toward Nicole. "Do you need to run off home right away today? If not, I was hoping you might join me for, er, *mellanmål*—I think your word is *snack*?" She smiled brightly. "Lunch was a long time ago, and I'm far too famished to wait for dinner."

Nicole hesitated. This was the first time Annike had come right out and invited her to do something specific. She didn't want to turn her down and appear rude. Besides, she wasn't particularly looking forward to rushing back to the Smiths' apartment, where she would have nothing to do for the rest of the afternoon but work on her homework, fend off Luc's advances, and listen to the kids shriek.

"Um, okay," she responded cautiously. "Do you want to go grab a burger or something?"

For the past two weeks Nicole had eaten lunch between classes at the McDonald's around the corner from school. Sometimes she went alone, though Ada had come with her once or twice, and she'd run into the Irish boys from her Artist's Eye class there a few times as well. Since Annike had her lunch break at a different hour,

Nicole had no idea if she liked the place or not.

Annike wrinkled her nose, effectively answering the question. "Ach, I'd rather not, if you don't mind. But what about that crêpe stand down the block?"

"Crêpes?" Nicole repeated uncertainly. "Um, I don't know if I would like something like that...."

"You mean you haven't tried a crêpe yet?" Annike's blue eyes widened in surprise. "Oh, but you really should, you know! They're *très bon*."

"Well..." Nicole hesitated.

Clearly taking that as assent, Annike smiled. "Great! Come on."

Nicole sighed. How many times had she wound up doing something she didn't really want to do just because someone else insisted? Zara never did anything she didn't want to do—in fact, she rarely did anything that wasn't actually her idea in the first place. Annie, too, was pretty good at saying thanks, but no thanks, as long as the person asking wasn't Zara.

Oh well, Nicole thought as she followed Annike. *If I don't like the looks of these crêpe thingies, I just won't eat one. No big deal.*

They headed down the block, dodging students, tourists, shoppers, and other people. "It's just ahead there," Annike said, pointing across the street.

As Nicole squinted at the quaint-looking food cart, which was labeled CRÊPERIE, she heard someone calling

Annike's name. A moment later a pair of girls their age caught up with them. One of them, petite and dark-haired, started chattering eagerly at Annike in what Nicole could only assume was Swedish.

Annike laughed and replied in the same language, then glanced apologetically at Nicole and the other girl. "Oh, sorry," she said. "Hey Petra, let's stick to English, okay?"

"Sorry!" The girl turned her bright smile in Nicole's direction. "My English not is so good as Annike's yet, sorry. I forget sometimes how to speak when too excited."

Annike introduced the girls. Petra was another Swede, though she and Annike had met only recently at their S.A.S.S. orientation. The other girl, Chloe, was an ivory-complexioned British brunette Nicole vaguely recognized from her large European-history class.

The two newcomers immediately accepted Annike's invitation to join them for crêpes. Nicole was tempted to make an excuse and slip away now that she wouldn't be leaving Annike all alone, but she couldn't quite find a break in the conversation. Petra was a chatterbox—she might not speak English as fluently as Annike, but that certainly didn't stop her from trying. With a pang of home-sickness Nicole realized Petra reminded her a little of her friend Patrice. Chloe didn't have as much to say, but occasionally tossed in a joke or other witty comment.

Nicole mostly listened in silence as the four of them stood in the line of waiting customers at the crêpe stand.

The menu hanging over the cart's service window was written in French. Nicole recognized quite a few of the words but didn't feel anywhere near confident enough to put them together into an actual order. And what if the crêpe guy didn't speak English? The thought of another encounter like the one in the bookstore made her shudder.

"Um, maybe I'll just wait while you guys eat," she said.

"Oh, no, please have a crêpe!" Annike exclaimed, clutching her arm. "You really ought to try one at least once. I'll pay if you like."

"Oh! No, it's not that, I…" Embarrassed, Nicole cleared her throat. "Um, I'm just not sure what to order, you know?"

"Do you fancy something sweet or savory?" Petra asked, staring intently at the menu board. "I can't myself decide; perhaps I will have one of both!"

"One of each," Annike corrected, then glanced toward Nicole for confirmation. "Correct?"

Nicole nodded, and Chloe smiled. "Poor Petra," she teased. "When she's hungry or excited, her tongue gets all twisted round those pesky English words."

Petra giggled. "It's not just English," she admitted. "I do the same in Swedish, too."

Chloe laughed, then glanced at Nicole. "You really ought to try a crêpe, you know," she said. "The food here is brilliant—I think it's my favorite takeaway stand in Paris so far. Think I'll go for the *fromage et champignon* again."

As Chloe and Petra discussed their choices, Nicole stared blankly at the menu board. "Shall I order for both of us?" Annike suggested to her tactfully. "After all, I'm forcing you to eat here, the least I can do is pick out something tasty for you, *ja*?"

Nicole smiled weakly. The odors drifting toward them from the crêpe stand *were* sort of tempting. "Sure," she said, pulling out a few euros and handing them to Annike. "Thanks. Um, something sweet would be good, I guess."

"Got it." Annike nodded, then stepped up to the counter, ordering rapidly in French.

Nicole hung back and watched as the other two girls gave their orders. Chloe seemed to be just as fluent in French as Annike, and while Petra struggled a little, her cheerful laugh at her own mistakes made the crêpe seller smile.

All three of them rejoined Nicole to wait for their food. For a minute or two the conversation revolved around the crêpes. Then it drifted to other subjects.

"I was certain I will die of frightened when I was to come here," Petra declared as they all took turns discussing their experiences in Paris so far.

"Fright," Chloe corrected. "You'd die of fright. And I felt the exact same way. I've never lived away from home before."

"Me, neither," Nicole blurted out. "It's so weird being here." She could hardly believe what she was hearing. These other girls all seemed so poised and sophisticated. Were they really just as nervous about all these new experiences as she was?

For a moment she almost felt comfortable with them. Then Annike shrugged and laughed. "Anyway, it's worth a little worry for the shopping alone, *ja*? Makes the Biblioteksgatan back in Stockholm look like a village flea market."

Nicole snapped back to reality. No, these girls weren't like her. Annike and Chloe both lived in big cities—Stockholm and London. Paris just wasn't as much of a stretch for them. As for Petra, well, she might talk as much as Patrice, but otherwise she seemed more like Zara or Nate—she had that same sort of automatic self-confidence.

Soon the crêpes were ready. Nicole cautiously accepted the paper plate Annike handed her, which held the neatly folded, cone-shaped crêpe. A bit of brown goo oozed from the seam at one end.

"Is that chocolate?" Nicole asked.

Annike smiled. "Just try it. *Bon appétit!*"

Nicole gingerly lifted one end of the folded crêpe and carefully bit into it. Her teeth tore easily through the warm, light shell, and a sweet, chocolaty taste filled her mouth.

"Whoa!" she cried, quickly chewing and swallowing the bite. "This is good!"

Petra and Chloe giggled. "You sound so surprised!" Chloe cried.

"I'm glad you like it. It's rather simple compared to some, but I thought it might be a good place to start," Annike told Nicole, sounding relieved. "It's just bananas and a bit of Nutella."

"Nutella?" Nicole said. "What's that? It tastes like chocolate."

"It *is* chocolate," Chloe put in. "It's a cocoa and hazel-nut spread—Nutella is the brand name. Don't you have it in the States?"

Nicole shrugged. "I don't know. But if we don't, we should!" She took another bite, chewing more slowly this time to savor the flavors.

Okay, so maybe there's at least one good thing about Paris after all, she thought. *Even Zara wouldn't be able to complain about this!*

From: Larsons9701@email.com
To: NicLar@email.com
Subject: Hello!

Dear Nicole,

Dad and I are happy to hear you enjoyed your crêpe experience yesterday. Those were one of my favorite things about Paris, too.

So we'd love to hear more about your other adventures as well! You haven't said much in your last few e-mails. Are classes going okay so far? How's your French coming along? It sounds like you're making some friends—that's good; we knew you would get along fine. You're stronger than you realize, I think. That's one reason we thought this trip would be so good for you.

In any case, I hope the crêpes will help you start to forgive us for sending you...wink, wink.

Love,
Mom

From: N8THEGR8@email.com
To: NicLar@email.com
Subject: Wut up?

Hey Nic,

Thanx 4 the reminder abt r anniversary next wk. Did u really think I'd 4get just cuz yur over there in frenchyland? Come on, gimme some credit! How could I 4get about the most beautiful girl in the world just cuz shez a few miles away turning on a bunch of frenchies instead of me????

Seriously tho, I'll b thinking abt u all day. Just like I do

every day. I can't wait til u get back and things r back 2 normal. Being apart sux.

Luv ya,

N

When she walked into the Smiths' apartment the next day
after school, Nicole found Mrs. Smith pulling on her coat
and looking harried.

"Oh, there you are, Nicole," the woman said distractedly, grabbing her purse and digging through it. "My editors
just called an urgent meeting and I really have to go, but
Luc isn't scheduled to be here for another hour and he's
not answering his cell phone at the moment. Could you do
me an enormous favor and watch the children until he
gets here? Normally I wouldn't impose on you, but—"

"Sure," Nicole interrupted. She was in a good mood—
not only had she received a particularly sweet e-mail from
Nate that morning, but her French teacher had returned
their latest quiz that day in her language class, and Nicole
had aced it. Plus she'd had lunch with Ada, Chloe, and
Petra, making her feel almost popular. "No problem," she
told Mrs. Smith magnanimously. "I'd love to help out."

"Oh, bless you!" Mrs. Smith looked relieved. "The twins
are asleep, so they shouldn't be any trouble at all...."

She rambled on for another moment or two, then hurried out the door, leaving Nicole alone with the children.

Brandon and Marissa had been sitting quietly on the sofa, but now they jumped to their feet.

"Play with us!" Brandon demanded.

Nicole smiled at him. Even Brandon's brattiness couldn't ruin her mood. Besides, he wasn't really such a bad kid—just overly exuberant. "What's the magic word?" she wheedled.

"Please!" Marissa spoke up. "Please-please-please!"

"That's right." Nicole patted the little girl on the head. "Okay, so what do you want to play?"

As the children scurried about pulling various toys and games off the shelves, she heard a thin wail from the back of the apartment. "Oops," Brandon said. "Sounds like one of the twins woke up."

"I'll take care of it." Nicole headed for the nursery/office, humming under her breath.

Someday I'll be doing this for real, she reminded herself with a happy shiver. She slowed to a stop, lost in the happy fantasy of her future family with Nate. A sudden loud squall snapped her out of it as the second twin joined voice with the first.

"All right, all right," she murmured, hurrying on. "I'm coming...."

"Bonjour," Luc called from the front door. "Anybody home?"

A moment later he walked into the living room. For a moment all Nicole could do was stare at him from where she'd just collapsed on the sofa. One twin was sleeping in the crook of her arm while the other chewed on a rattle at her feet. Across the room, Brandon and Marissa were arguing over a box of crayons.

"Thank God," she gasped out at last. "What took you so long?"

"Sorry I am a little late, but the *métro*...Hey, what happened in here, anyway? The place looks like a disaster."

Nicole pushed herself to a more upright position, being careful not to jostle the sleeping baby. "How do you do it?" she blurted out. "How can you stand to stay trapped here in this apartment with four little kids to look after?" She was vaguely aware of Marissa shooting her an insulted glance, but ignored it.

Luc shrugged. "Ah, but it is my job," he said. "Besides, I'm quite fond of the little rascals. I amuse them, they amuse me, and then at the end of the day I go home. It suits me fine."

"Well, I thought it would suit me, too. That's why I said yes when Mrs. Smith asked if I'd babysit." Nicole shook her head. "But it's totally insane! I thought taking care of kids was fun, but they had me running all over the place nonstop without two seconds to even sit down and breathe. It's nothing like I thought it would be."

Luc kept a straight face, though there was an amused twinkle in his eyes. "Well, you are free now," he said. "I'll take care of it."

Free. The word rushed through Nicole like a stiff breeze, giving her a sudden jolt of energy. She was free. She didn't have to stay there chained to the Smith children for one minute longer.

She could do anything she wanted. The truth of that statement filled her with relief. She hurried over and handed the baby she was holding to Luc. Then, impulsively, she gave them both a hug.

As she pulled back she winced, expecting some kind of smart or flirtatious comment from Luc. But he only smiled at her.

"Okay, then," he said, turning toward the older kids. "Have you little monsters had a snack yet?"

Brandon and Marissa immediately dropped their crayons and leaped to their feet. "Snack! Snack! Snack!" they chanted excitedly, swarming around Luc.

"Want to join us, Nicole?" Luc asked. "I make quite a good snack chef, if I say so myself."

His voice and eyes were so friendly that for a moment Nicole was tempted. When he wasn't trying to flirt with her, he wasn't such a bad guy. In fact, he was pretty cool.

Then Marissa let out a particularly loud shriek, and Nicole quickly shook her head. "Thanks, maybe another time," she said. "I—I really want to get out for a while."

She rushed for the door, barely pausing long enough to grab her jacket. Once she emerged from the building into the crisp afternoon air, she took several deep breaths, a little surprised at how relieved she was to be out there. What was the big deal? Was she really so freaked out by spending an hour or so watching a few little kids?

Yes, she admitted to herself. *I guess I was.*

She wandered slowly down the block, not really paying attention to where she was going. She was too busy trying to figure out what it was that had wigged her out so much. So the Smith kids hadn't exactly fit into her homey, rose-colored fantasies of the future....

The truth clicked into place in her mind like the last piece of a difficult puzzle. That was it, wasn't it? Her image of what it would be like to be grown-up and married to Nate and raising children had always seemed so perfect. But just now, for the first time, she had realized that the true day-to-day reality of that sort of thing could be a lot more complicated.

I guess I never really thought about it before, she told herself. *I figured it's just what people do—they fall in love, get married, have kids. It should be a no-brainer, right?*

She sighed, vowing not to think about it anymore. It would just make her crazy, and she definitely didn't need that, especially now that she was starting to feel a little more comfortable being in Paris.

Because really, all she had to do was survive the rest of the semester, maybe try to have a decent time if possible. Then she could go home and let her life get back to normal. She could figure out the rest later.

Chapter Six

From: NicLar@email.com

To: PatriceQT@email.com; ZZZar@email.com;
   anniegood@email.com

Subject: My life as a Parisian (part 9,432)

Hey guys, what up?

So I'm lying on my bed & can't move anything but my fingers, cuz I had2 walk all over Paris 2day on a field trip.
Ugh! I think my muscles r in shock.

But anyway, the trip was sorta interesting. U might think there's not much 2 see here other than, like, the Eiffel Tower and some boring museums or whatever, but there is. Anyway, I'll tell u about it some other time when I'm more awake.

Cuz 4 now, I'm 2 busy thinking abt N & our anniversary. I can't b-lieve I won't b there 2 celebrate w/him in person this yr!!! Total bummer...U guys will have 2 show him pix of me that day 2 remind him of me...**sniff, sob!**

j/k. I'm sure we'll survive. At least we can talk on the phone & stuff. It just sux, u know? (I know u do...)

Miss you all!!!
Luv,
Nic

"Did your feet recover from yesterday yet?" Annike asked with a grin as Nicole walked into their Artist's Eye classroom. It was the day after the latest class field trip, and most of the students were still buzzing about it.

Nicole let out a dramatic groan and flopped into the empty seat beside Annike. "Feet? What feet?" she exclaimed. "All I have left are stumps."

Annike laughed. "I know. It was a lot of walking, wasn't it? Especially in the cemetery—it's so huge! Like a little city of mausoleums or something."

"Yeah." Nicole sat up a little straighter and glanced at her. "You know, I never would've guessed a field trip to a cemetery could be interesting. But it totally was, wasn't it? I mean, to think about all those famous people."

She shuddered slightly, thinking back to the class's first stop, the Cimetière du Père Lachaise, an enormous Parisian cemetery where lots of famous people were buried, including Jim Morrison, Oscar Wilde, Marcel Proust, Frédéric Chopin, Georges Seurat, Gertrude Stein, and countless other writers, artists, statesmen, and famous people. The class had spent a long time wandering along the tree-lined walkways peering at stone grave markers, square, solemn sarcophagi, and other memorials.

"I know what you mean." Annike grinned, her blue eyes twinkling. "Then again, visiting a cemetery started to seem quite normal once we found out where we were going next!"

Nicole laughed. After they'd finished at Père Lachaise, Dr. Morley had explained that they still had another stop to make on their trip. They'd ended up at, of all places, the Paris Sewer Museum! That had meant still more walking as they hurried through the rather odoriferous displays, reading the signs and looking at the huge pipes and tunnels that carried waste material beneath Paris. By the time they made their way back to school, Nicole's feet were throbbing. She was pretty sure she'd never walked so much in a single day—and that included the time the previous summer when she'd completed a charity walkathon sponsored by Nate's father's office.

"Yeah, my friends back home will freak when they hear about the sewer museum," she said. "Annie can't even use a public restroom without practically fainting from disgust. Then there's Nate...." She giggled, imagining her boyfriend's reaction.

"What?" Annike asked. "What's so funny?"

"Oh, it's just that Nate is just such a, well, a typical *boy*, you know?" Nicole shrugged. "He likes jokes about poop and stuff—like a little kid. He and his friends would've gone nuts at a place like that." She couldn't help laughing out loud as she pictured it. "He cracks me up when he gets going on something like that. Not because the jokes are that funny, really—he just gets such a kick out of them, you know?"

Annike smiled. "Nate sounds like quite a character."

"Oh, he is." Nicole sighed, her smile fading. "I miss him. Especially now—did I tell you today is our anniversary?"

"You mentioned it a few times," Annike said. "I guess it will be especially difficult for you being apart on this day, yes?"

"Definitely." Nicole bit her lip. "I'm trying not to stress about it too much, though. It's not like I can do anything about it. Anyway, Nate and I are already planning to blow all our extra funds on an extra-long anniversary phone call tonight. I can't wait! It's hard to believe I've only talked to him twice since I've been here."

"Yes, I know," Annike said. "I have only spoken with my parents three times. It is very strange, isn't it? Being away from home."

"Yeah." Nicole picked at the corner of the school desk. "It's weird, though. At first that was all I thought about— how bizarre it was to be here, how much I missed home and the people there, that kind of stuff. But now, some-times..."

"You forget all that and just go like the flow, as if it wasn't strange at all to be here?" Annike nodded. "Me, too. I was just thinking about that yesterday when we were leaving the Père Lachaise." She shrugged. "I almost said something to you about it—I guess I was afraid you wouldn't understand."

"Oh, I understand." Nicole smiled at her, grateful to have found someone so much on the same wavelength. "Totally."

At that moment Dr. Morley strode into the room and called for attention. Nicole got up and headed back to her own desk, feeling less stressed than usual about being there—Artist's Eye, school, Paris in general.

Maybe it's true what Dad told me in that e-mail the other day, she mused as the teacher started talking. *People can get used to almost anything.*

She expected Dr. Morley to spend most of the class period discussing the previous day's field trip. Instead she quickly realized that the teacher was announcing a new class-participation activity.

Nicole sat up a little straighter, suddenly anxious. She hated class participation-type activities. Standing up in front of a classful of bored faces for any reason whatsoever always gave her major flashbacks to her all-too-frequent grand entrances to a new school. She'd managed to stay in the background for Dr. Morley's class activities so far, but she knew that lucky streak probably wouldn't last much longer.

Dr. Morley was already explaining the exercise. "...and yesterday we spent time looking at things many people might not consider—well, hello, Ms. Williamson. So glad you could join us."

Nicole glanced toward the door just in time to see Ada scurry into the room. "Sorry, sorry!" the tall Australian girl cried breathlessly. "I'm so sorry I'm late!"

"It's quite all right. Take your seat." The teacher paused as Ada rushed toward her desk.

Ada shot Nicole a wink and a grin as she took her seat. Nicole waggled her fingers to return the greeting, though she was still distracted by Dr. Morley's announcement. What kind of class activity was in store for them?

Dr. Morley continued. "As I was saying, we saw things yesterday that most people might not consider fit for public viewing," she said. "But a true artist has different ways of seeing even the most ordinary or humble things—not taking them for granted as most people do."

"Yeah, like seein' the special beauty of Parisian poo!"

Seamus called out in his distinctive Irish accent, making the whole class laugh.

Dr. Morley smiled at him. "Just for that, young man, I think we'll let you go first." As Seamus groaned melodramatically, pretending to be upset, the teacher stepped over to her desk and picked up a soft black felt hat. "I've put slips of paper in this hat. Each of you will choose one, and then you must get the class to guess the place or item on your slip by describing it the way an artist might see it—without using any giveaway words, of course. Understand?"

The class murmured its comprehension. When Nicole glanced around, most of her fellow students looked intrigued, even excited, about the assignment. She felt her stomach sink as she rapidly calculated the time left in the hour and the likelihood that they would run out of it before her turn came. Unfortunately, with only thirteen people in the class, it seemed almost certain she would have to take a turn.

Seamus got up and ambled to the front of the room. "Pick something cracker, mate!" his friend Finn called to him, making the class laugh again.

"Silly clown," Annike said with a grin. "I hope you get something dull like 'traffic light' when it's your turn. Would serve you right!"

Finn merely grinned in response. Meanwhile Seamus was already reaching into the hat. He pulled out a slip of paper and glanced at it.

"Crikey!" he exclaimed, bringing still more laughter. "All right, all right. Pay attention, you lot....Here goes."

He started dancing, kicking up his legs as high as he could in a rather spastic imitation of a cancan dancer. At the same time, he held both hands out from his chest to indicate a rather large bosom.

"I know!" Finn called out as the rest of the class, including Nicole, collapsed with laughter. "It's that place with the windmill, you know, where the birds kick up their heels and show their knickers...."

"The Moulin Rouge," Ada supplied.

Dr. Morley's expression remained stern, though there was a twinkle in her eyes. "That's correct, my dear. But we're not supposed to be playing charades here, Seamus," she scolded. "Now choose another slip—and this time, I want to hear some words!"

"Yeah, stop acting the maggot and grow up!" Finn added helpfully.

Seamus good-naturedly pulled another slip. "All right, all right," he murmured. "Er, if I were an *artiste*"—he slipped into an exaggerated French pronunciation of the last word—"I might say that this item is all smooth lines and shiny surfaces, smaller than its relatives but handy for tight spots. The smart armor of its outsides hides its black, active interior."

"The Eiffel Tower?" a British guy named Michael guessed hopefully.

Seamus shook his head. "This thing can be necessary for those quick trips down to the boozer or just to wrap yer legs around for fun...."

That brought out a few more guesses from Finn and others, most of them dirty. But Seamus shook his head at every one.

"Not even close, any of you," he said. "Let me try again—one must feed this thing with liquid gold or it won't do a thing for you."

Most of the class looked blank, but Nicole tentatively raised her hand. "Is it—are you talking about those little motor scooters everyone rides around here?"

"That's it!" Seamus pumped his fist. "Give that lady a prize!"

Dr. Morley chuckled. "Good job this time, Seamus. And very nicely solved, Nicole," she said. "Since you seem to be good at this little game, why don't you give it a go next?"

Nicole gulped, wishing she'd kept her big mouth shut. "Er, that's okay," she mumbled. "I don't really..."

But the teacher was already shaking the hat, gesturing for her to come forward. Not knowing how to refuse, Nicole reluctantly left her seat and walked to the front of the room.

"Luck!" Annike whispered as she passed.

The slip of paper Nicole drew out of the hat contained two words: PARIS MÉTRO. She grimaced at the irony— though the *métro* no longer terrified her, she still hated every moment she spent in its dank, dark, dirty environs.

"Go on, my dear," Dr. Morley said encouragingly as Nicole stood staring at the piece of paper.

"Oh," Nicole said. "Okay, um..."

She bit her lip, trying to figure out what to say. But her mind was completely blank. How would an artist see the *métro*? She couldn't imagine seeing it as anything other than an affordable and practical, yet disgusting means of transportation. She felt her cheeks start to go red as everyone stared at her.

"Er, this is a thing that you can use to get around," she stammered uncertainly. "You can see it from underneath the ground or the top part of the *métro* stop—oops!"

Her hands flew to her face and she stopped. She started to apologize, but Dr. Morley didn't seem upset at all.

"Never mind, Nicole," the teacher said soothingly as Nicole sat down. "I'm aware that this exercise isn't as easy as it might seem. But let's not move on just yet; this is an interesting one to discuss, I think." She turned to the rest of the class. "I'm sure you've all experienced the Paris *métro* by now. Millions of people use it to get around every day and probably never think twice about it. Who here can come up with a different way of looking at it?"

Several students raised their hands. The teacher called on Annike.

"The *métro* reminds me of a sort of city within the city," Annike said. "It's separate from the surface world in many

ways—it's got its own weather, sort of. At least you don't know what the weather is outdoors when you're down there, you know? You cannot even tell what time of day it is. It might just as well be another planet."

Other hands were already waving as she finished. It seemed that everyone was eager to share his or her own impressions of the *métro*.

At first Nicole was too aware of her mistake to pay much attention. But gradually she got caught up in her classmates' views of the *métro*. One girl described the way it looked on maps as a multiheaded snake slithering its way around Paris. Another said the muted colors of the dimmer sections of the stations, together with the ageless architecture of the tunnels, reminded her of an antique black-and-white photo that had been partially colorized. Even Finn contributed the opinion that the *métro* was the perfect stage on which to observe the theory of survival of the fittest in action, and therefore could be called the true urban jungle.

Nicole found herself nodding along with several of the comments, realizing that they made a lot of sense. *Cool,* she thought. *Maybe this class isn't as lame as I thought....*

For the first time ever, Nicole was smiling as she emerged from the *métro* station near the Smiths' apartment. Thinking about the class discussion earlier that day had made the less pleasant smells, sounds, and other aspects of her commute a bit more bearable—almost exotic, even. *Maybe Dr. Morley was right,* she thought as she blinked in the afternoon sunshine. *Maybe this artist's-eye stuff is useful for more than just school. At least a little.*

That reminded her about the assignment Dr. Morley had given them at the end of class. They were supposed to take what they'd learned that day and use it as a framework to write about the previous day's field trip in their journals.

Realizing she was approaching a neighborhood café where she'd eaten once or twice with the Smiths, Nicole decided to stop in for a while and work on her journal there. The place had English-speaking waiters, an excellent selection of herbal teas, and a low-key atmosphere. Besides, she had a few hours to kill before she could call Nate during his lunch hour.

Since the afternoon was warm, she found a seat at one of the outdoor tables on the sidewalk just outside the front door. After ordering a cup of tea, she pulled out her journal. Soon she was completely absorbed in her writing.

"*Ça va,* Nicole?" a voice spoke after a while, interrupting her train of thought.

Before she quite realized what she was doing, Nicole answered the greeting in French: "*Ça va bien.*"

She glanced up to see Luc standing over her wearing a delighted grin. "Ah! So she can speak something other than straight American."

Normally Luc's teasing irritated her like crazy. But somehow today she was able to hear it a little differently— as good-natured ribbing between friends. Potential friends, at least. She returned his smile, trying not to notice how cute he looked in his jeans and black sweater.

"I guess the secret's out," she said. "I was trying to keep my French-speaking talent from everyone, but you found me out."

He chuckled and gestured to the empty chair across from her. "May I join you?"

"Sure," she said, feeling unusually friendly toward him, though she wasn't really sure why. If she could see the *métro* differently, why not Luc?

He sat down and gestured for a waiter, ordering himself a coffee. Then he nodded at her journal, which was still open on the table. "What are you doing?"

She draped one arm over the page, feeling a little embarrassed. "It's a class assignment," she said. "See, we're supposed to be keeping these artist's journals talking about the stuff we do in class. Right now we're supposed to be writing our impressions of the field trip we took yesterday."

"Cool." Luc leaned across the table and tapped her hand, which was still covering the journal page. "So what are you writing?"

Nicole blushed a little. It seemed like sort of an intimate

question. "I—I don't know," she said. "I guess I'm just writing down whatever comes to mind."

"I see," Luc leaned back in his seat. "So this trip of yours, where did you go? To the Louvre? The Musée D'Orsay?"

"No." Nicole grinned. "We went to the Père Lachaise cemetery and, um, the sewer museum."

Luc blinked. Then he laughed. "Ah," he said. "So now you must write something meaningful about—er, what is it in English? Poo?"

Nicole giggled. "Right. It's a very intellectual assignment. So do you guys talk about this kind of stuff in your college classes?"

"Sadly, no." Luc glanced up as an attractive young waitress brought his coffee. *"Merci, chérie,"* he said, flashing her a rather wicked smile, quickly adding something in French that made the waitress blush and roll her eyes. She responded just as quickly.

Nicole's French was getting better every day, but she couldn't quite follow what either of them had said. "What did you just say to her?" she asked when the waitress moved out of earshot.

Luc grinned and reached for the sugar. "I mentioned that her beautiful body was in danger of making me spill my hot coffee. Then she told me what she thought I should do with my coffee."

Nicole wasn't sure whether to be amused or appalled. "So that kind of line works for you?"

"No." Luc stirred his coffee and took a sip. He winked at her over the edge of the cup. "Don't look so scandalized, *chérie*. That waitress and I, we are old friends. It was nothing but a joke."

"So, a sense of humor," Nicole commented. "That's a good quality in a guy." Not wanting him to think she was flirting with him, she quickly added, "Nate has a great sense of humor. It's one of the first things I loved about him."

Luc gazed at her. "Humor is important. It is one of the things that makes us human, I think. What else do you see in your Nate?"

"Oh, I don't know." Nicole wasn't particularly comfortable with the way the conversation was headed all of a sudden. Even though Luc was being nice, she didn't quite trust his motives. "I love just about everything about him. But hey, I thought we were supposed to be talking about school, remember? I keep answering all your questions, but you never tell me anything about yourself."

She meant to sound light and humorous, but it came out sounding a little like an accusation. Fortunately, Luc didn't seem disturbed by it.

"What would you like to know about me?" He spread both hands over the table, palms up. "I am an open book."

"Just anything." Nicole shrugged. "What are you studying in your college classes?"

"Mostly business subjects," Luc replied, taking another sip of coffee. "I wish I could take more classes about poo and such, as you do at the international school. However, I cannot pay for many classes each semester, and my mother, she cannot afford to help me very much, and so I must be practical."

"Oh. So is that why you're working as the Smiths' nanny?"

"Indeed," he replied. "I am lucky to have this kind of job. The Smiths, they are happy to work around my schedule. As you know, I am there four days per week, including once on the weekend. It seems to work well for all of us so far, and I hope to continue there as long as possible. Perhaps until I finish my studies, if the Smiths remain in Paris that long."

"That's cool." Nicole couldn't help being impressed by how open Luc was being.

Maybe it wasn't that he didn't want to talk about himself before now, she thought guiltily. *Maybe it's just that I wasn't interested in listening.*

He was gazing at her across the table, looking completely relaxed. She stared back, wondering what sorts of thoughts really went on behind those intense green eyes.

"So with your job and your schoolwork, how do you

have time to sit around in cafés talking over coffee?" she asked him, half-playful and half-serious.

He smiled. "Work and school, they are important. But it is also important to have fun. Otherwise, what is the point of living?" He took a sip of coffee. "What do you do for fun back home in America?"

"Oh, the usual stuff. Hanging out with Nate and my friends, going to the movies, listening to music..."

They spent the next twenty minutes or so chatting about pop culture and other casual topics. It wasn't until Luc checked his watch and mentioned that he had to be going soon that Nicole realized she'd drained three cups of tea while the sun set and the streetlights winked on.

"Oops," she said, suddenly realizing she'd totally lost track of the time. It was almost late enough to try reaching Nate. "Guess I'd better go, too. I almost forgot—"

She cut herself off abruptly, causing Luc to glance at her curiously. "What is it? I hope I did not make you late for something important. A hot date, perhaps?" He winked playfully.

"No, it's no big deal." Nicole grabbed her backpack from under the table, tucking her class journal and pen into it. As friendly as their chat had been, she didn't feel like sharing her anniversary news with Luc. She could take some teasing, but not about that. "It's just that the Smiths will be wondering where I am. It's almost dinnertime."

Luc called for the waitress again. "I'll get it," he said when the check arrived.

Nicole hesitated only slightly before nodding. "Thanks."

As they wandered out of the café, she shot him a side-long glance. It was strange to realize that she'd actually had a nice time talking with him. Maybe she'd been wrong about him.

He's no Nate, of course, she thought as she waved good-bye to him on the corner. *But maybe he's not so bad in his own French-guy kind of way....*

She was still musing over her encounter with Luc as she entered the Smiths' apartment a few minutes later. Mr. Smith was sitting on the living-room floor playing blocks with the two older kids.

He glanced up with a smile. "Hey there, Nicole," he said. "How was your day?"

"Pretty good." Nicole almost mentioned running into Luc. But she didn't want Mr. Smith to get any funny ideas about the two of them. "A couple of my classes were kind of interesting today."

Marissa looked up from her toys. "I went to tumbling class today!" she announced proudly.

"That's right," Mr. Smith said, patting Marissa on the head. Then he glanced at Nicole again. "By the way, my wife just called—she's running a little late, but she's going

to pick up some takeout on her way home. She's expecting to be here in an hour or so. I hope you're not too hungry to wait."

"I'm too hungry!" Brandon yelled.

"It's okay," Nicole said, raising her voice to be heard over the little boy's shouts. "That will give me time to call Nate before dinner. It's our anniversary today and we set up a phone date."

"Oh! How nice." Mr. Smith smiled. "Go on, then. I'll try to keep the kids quiet so you two can hear each other."

"Thanks." Nicole turned and hurried toward her room.

Pushing away all lingering thoughts about Luc, she focused on the coming phone call. She'd been looking forward to it all week—no, longer than that. E-mails were fine, but they just couldn't replace a real conversation sometimes. Especially on an important day like today.

Closing the bedroom door, she grabbed the phone and quickly dialed Nate's number. She pressed it to her ear, taking a few deep breaths to try to quiet her own pounding heart. Soon, soon she would hear his familiar voice in her ear, telling her he loved her....

There was a click, and then his voice answered: "Yo, this is Nate. You know how this works, so go for it." *Beep!*

Voice mail. Nicole pulled the phone away from her ear and blinked at it. Then she put it to her ear again.

"Nate?" she said into it, wondering if this was one of his

jokes—pretending to be his own voice mail to trick her into thinking he'd forgotten.

But it was really the voice mail. Shaking her head, Nicole hung up and quickly punched in the number again, with the same result.

Hanging up again without leaving a message, Nicole glanced at the clock on her bedside table. Maybe it was still too early—school rules back home dictated that all student cell phones had to stay off during class time. If Nate had to stay behind to talk to a teacher or something, he might not have turned his phone back on yet.

She waited five minutes, watching the seconds tick past on the old-fashioned alarm clock on her bedside table. But when she finally allowed herself to dial, she once again heard nothing but Nate's voice-mail message on the other end of the line. This time she waited for the beep and then spoke, trying not to sound as panicky and confused as she felt.

"Hey Nate, it's Nicole. Happy anniversary, sweetie!" She clutched the phone tightly. "Um, I keep trying to call you for our phone date, but you're not picking up....Hope nothing's wrong or whatever. I'll try back again. Um, hope to talk to you soon. I love you."

She hung up, feeling tears tickle the corners of her eyes. Where was he? How could he have forgotten their anniversary call?

Chapter Seven

From: N8THEGR8@email.com

To: NicLar@email.com

Subject: SORRY SORRY SORRY!!!!

Nic! I'm such a big loser—I can't b-lieve I 4got r fone call earlier! U know it's not cuz of u. I'm just a dork that's all, u know?

Anyway, I hope u can 4give me. I swear I'll make it up 2 u, ok? Pleeeeese say u're not mad? I couldn't stand it if I messed up enuf 2 make the most b-u-tiful girl in the world mad at me 4 good...

N

"So he apologized, hmm?" Annike asked as she and Nicole strolled toward the *métro* stop after school a couple of days later. It was unseasonably warm for October, and they were taking their time to enjoy the weather. "So does that mean he's, um, what's the phrase one would use in America? Off the hook?"

"Yeah." Nicole shrugged. "I mean, I wish he'd remembered so we could have talked on our anniversary like we planned. But I'm not going to hassle him about it too much. What's the point? I already knew he's not exactly Mr. Detail-Oriented. I guess he just got caught up in talking to his friends or whatever and forgot to switch on his phone when he went to lunch. It's not like he blew me off on purpose or anything."

Nicole forced a smile. It still hurt a little to think about how Nate had forgotten—she just couldn't help it. But she'd already decided it wasn't worth getting mad at him over something like that. They'd made plans to have their nice, long conversation that weekend to make up for the missed call, and she wanted to spend that time talking rather than fighting.

Annike was giving her a searching look. "Are you sure

you are okay with it now?" she asked. "You still look upset."

"I guess I am a little," Nicole admitted. "But I'll get over it. At least I have a lot going on here to distract me."

That much was true. Over the past couple of weeks Nicole's life had settled into a not entirely unpleasant rhythm. She was doing well in her classes and keeping up with her homework. After school she sometimes hung out with Annike and Ada and other new friends, including the talkative Swedish girl, Petra; Ada's fellow Aussie, Janet; and a few others. She became a semiregular at the *crêperie* down the street. Occasionally she stopped in at Marie and Renaud's apartment for tea and a chat or a game of cards. Evenings and weekends were punctuated with frequent e-mail exchanges with her family, friends, and of course Nate, who had sent at least five apologetic e-mails in the two days since their anniversary.

"Well, I just hope he appreciates you," Annike declared. They had reached the *métro* stop, and she paused and turned to face Nicole. "A lot of girlfriends might not be so faithful as you if they found themselves here in Paris."

"I guess." For some reason, Luc's face popped into Nicole's mind. She made a face, irritated with herself for the random thought. Why in the world should he come into her mind during a discussion about Nate?

Maybe because Luc turned out to be more a part of my anniversary than Nate was? she thought ruefully.

"What's wrong?" Annike asked, noticing her expression.

"Nothing." As close as she and Annike were becoming, Nicole didn't want to share her thoughts about Luc at the moment. "Um, I just wish you didn't have that history paper to write tonight, so we could go do something."

Annike groaned. "You had to remind me, didn't you? I suppose that's my cue to get going. I'll see you tomorrow."

"See you then." Nicole watched as Annike hurried down the steps and veered off toward the right. Nicole turned left and headed for the train back to the Smiths' neighborhood.

When she let herself into the apartment a short time later, she found Luc waiting for her. The Smiths were nowhere to be seen.

"It's a gorgeous afternoon, and I've got the rest of it off," Luc announced without preamble. "What say we go see some sights? You've still barely seen any of Paris, you know."

"What are you talking about?" she joked, slinging her school bag onto a chair. "I've seen the sewer museum. What more could there be?"

He grinned. "I have the perfect place to start. It's a bit touristy," he warned. "But still one of my favorite spots in Paris. I think you might like it, too."

"We'll see about that," Nicole teased. "This isn't some restaurant where you're going to try to trick me into eating snails or something, is it?"

"*Oublions le passé.* Trust me."

They were out the door and halfway to the *métro* stop before Nicole realized Luc hadn't really given her a chance to say no. Okay, so maybe he and Nate had something in common after all, she thought wryly, flashing back to the time Nate had impulsively decided they should go bowling instead of driving all the way to Washington to use his parents' spare symphony tickets. Nicole had ended up eating nachos and throwing spares in her best dress and panty hose. That was Nate—he didn't like to feel too tied down by plans and preparations, preferring to live his life at the spur of the moment. Sometimes that could be annoying, like when he forgot their anniversary or bagged out on something she really wanted to do. Other times it could be exhilarating, making Nicole feel like all the two of them really needed to be happy was each other.

Thinking about Nate was making her homesick again, so she pushed such thoughts out of her mind. She would be home with him again soon enough. In the meantime, she might as well take a lesson from him and enjoy the adventure—at least a little.

"Wow." Nicole shaded her eyes against the strong rays of the setting sun. "What is that thing?"

Luc grinned, seeming pleased by her reaction. "What do you think? Rather cool, isn't it? Do you like?"

"I—I'm not sure." Nicole stared at the odd sight in front of her. She and Luc were standing at one end of a large public fountain filled with more than a dozen colorful modern sculptures, most of them moving or spitting water or both.

She stared from one sculpture to another. Each seemed more outlandish than the last—the cartoonish reclining mermaid; a plump little heart shooting water straight up in a graceful arc; an anxious-looking elephant head; a rather creepy-looking skull-like face set high atop a jumble of dark metal; a pair of bright red lips spitting water. And near the center stood the largest sculpture of all—a giant, multicolored bird? Nicole wasn't quite sure what it was supposed to be. It reminded her a little of the bright crayon drawings the Smith kids liked to make and stick on the refrigerator.

Luc seemed amused. "A lot of people have the same reaction." He waved a hand at the dozens of others standing or sitting nearby, most of whom were also staring at the artwork. "It's known as the Stravinsky Fountain, after the famous composer. The pieces are supposed to represent some of his works."

"Really? That's kind of cool. But which work is that supposed to be?" Nicole pointed to the spitting lips.

"Ah, you caught me." Luc laughed. "I do not know much about Stravinsky or his music." He shrugged and smiled. "I just like the fountain."

"What?" Nicole put a hand to her heart, pretending to be shocked. "You mean you don't know absolutely everything there is to know about *Paris*?" She pronounced the city's name with an exaggerated French accent.

He jumped to his feet and stuck out his hand. "Come," he said with a grin. "We shall take your mind off your great disappointment in me by taking some pictures in front of the fountain. You will want to show your friends back home what you have been doing with yourself while here, no?"

Nicole shrugged. "Good idea. But I didn't bring my camera."

"No problem." With a flourish, Luc pulled a small disposable camera out of his jacket pocket. "As we say here in France, *voilà*!"

They spent the next twenty minutes getting passersby to take their picture as they struck silly poses in front of the sculptures. Nicole pretended to be pushing Luc into the fountain, struck sultry poses near the mermaid, or stood at the edge of the water and spread her arms, imitating the bird-thing in the background. If her friends back home could see her now, she suspected they would think she was crazy. But just at the moment, she didn't care.

Finally, Luc took the camera from an amused though befuddled German tourist and checked the readout. "Just one photo left," he told Nicole. "Go on and do something— I'll be the photographer this time."

"Okay, I've got an idea." Nicole scrambled around the fountain, looking for the right angle. With some guidance from Luc, she finally figured out exactly where she had to crouch so that she could purse her lips and, when Luc angled the camera just right, appear to be giving the lip sculpture a big smooch.

"Got it!" Luc called to her as he snapped the shutter.

"Cool!" Breathless and pink-cheeked, Nicole danced back to him, still laughing at her own goofiness. "I can't wait to see how that one turns out."

"Yes." Luc's smile was suddenly sly and a little dangerous. "Of course, if it's kissing you are after, I know a much easier way to go about it."

Nicole blushed. Lately, Luc had cut back a little on the overt flirting. But once in a while he still caught her off guard with a comment or even just one of those piercing looks. Sort of like the way he was looking at her right now.

"Hey, I'm starved," she said brightly, suddenly very eager to change the subject. "Are any of these cafés any good?"

Luc accepted the abrupt change of subject good-naturedly, as always. "But of course," he said. "In Paris, all cafés are good."

Soon they were seated at an outdoor table sipping coffee and people-watching. Nicole's gaze wandered toward the huge, odd-looking building nearby.

"What's that place?" she asked, pointing.

"It is the Georges Pompidou Center," Luc replied. "A museum of modern art and culture. I am surprised you have not visited it yet on one of your class trips. It is famous not only for the artwork within, but for the avant-garde architecture of the building itself. As a child, I called it the inside-out museum—see how the pipes and stair-cases and things are visible from the exterior?"

Nicole stirred her coffee. "I'm sure we'll get there at some point," she said. "It sounds like just the kind of place Dr. Morley would love."

Luc smiled. "Yes, it sounds that way from things you have said. I know it impressed me from the first time I went there as a schoolboy. Of course the reason is probably that I was so impressed to see that one of the displays was an ordinary toilet hanging on the wall."

As he spoke, Nicole watched his face. Now that she was getting to know him a little better, it was easier to tell when he was joking around and when he was being more serious. But this time she wasn't completely sure.

"A toilet?" she repeated uncertainly.

Luc nodded. "A urinal, to be more specific," he said. "It is a well-known piece by Duchamp."

"Hmm." Toilets on display in a museum? Nicole won-dered what public-toilet-phobic Annie would think about something like that.

Just then a pretty young waitress passed by their table.

"S'il vous plaît," Luc called to her, then said a few more lines to her in French. Nicole was fairly sure the first part had something to do with getting more coffee. But the rest sounded suspiciously like a compliment on the girl's striking green eyes and long legs.

"What was that all about?" she inquired when the waitress moved on, remembering his comments at the café the other day. "Do you know her, too?"

"Non." He waggled his eyebrows mischievously. "But I would like to." He grinned. "Jealous?"

"Don't be silly." Nicole glanced down into her coffee cup, willing herself not to blush. It wasn't the first time she'd noticed the way Luc flirted with just about every female he encountered. It seemed to be his way of being friendly. Was that all he was doing with her, or was there something more to it? And why did she care what some random French guy thought of her anyway?

But he wasn't just a random French guy anymore. That was the problem. He had started to become a real person to her—an individual with his own set of pluses and minuses, just like all the people back home.

Sort of like Paris itself, she mused thoughtfully, stirring a little more sugar into her coffee and glancing out at the busy plaza. She still didn't really want to be there, but at least now she could see the good points about it—stuff like this weirdly cool fountain, and all the great shopping, and yummy crêpes on every corner, and people like

Annike and Marie and Renaud and yes, even Luc.

"Well, you don't need to be jealous, *ma chérie*," Luc said, breaking into her thoughts. "You know you are always beauty number one to me."

She blinked at him. Despite her earlier thoughts, she realized she couldn't quite tell if he was joking or not this time, either.

What if he wasn't? The little flutter in her stomach at the thought made her gulp nervously. This wasn't supposed to be happening—she definitely wasn't supposed to be having warm fuzzy feelings about Luc. What about Nate?

The thought made her feel guilty. She was probably just taking out her anger about the anniversary thing in some weird way by noticing Luc. Totally immature.

"Hey, it's getting late," she blurted out, pushing away her coffee cup and glancing at her watch. "I should probably get home before the Smiths think I ran away or something."

"All right, then." Luc smiled at her. "You can find your own way home, *n'est-ce pas*?"

"Sure." Nicole smiled. "I'm an old pro at the *métro* these days. No problem at all."

"Good. Then I will stay here, and perhaps make a new friend." Luc inclined his head in the direction of the pretty waitress, who was serving a nearby table.

"Um, sure." Nicole realized she was blushing slightly, though she wasn't quite sure why. "See you later."

"À bientôt."

Nicole hurried away from the table. She liked Luc—he was a cool, smart, fun guy. A good friend. So why did hanging out with him always leave her feeling flustered and weirded out?

She was still fretting over her fun but confusing afternoon with Luc as she entered the apartment a little while later. Mr. Smith was sitting on the sofa reading a book to the two older kids.

"Hi, Nicole," he greeted her. "You missed a call a little while ago. I didn't catch it myself—was in the middle of giving the babies a bath. But I left it for you on the machine. Sounded like a young man."

Her heart jumped. "Really?" she said. "Thanks!"

She raced to the answering machine in the kitchen. where the message light was blinking rapidly. She pressed the button and Nate's familiar voice poured out of the tiny speakers, sounding distant and tinny.

"Hey, beautiful," he said. "It's me—surprise! And this time you're the one who's not home! So we're even, right?" He laughed. "Listen, I'm calling because I just had a great idea. I found out we have a day off school in a couple of weeks for a teachers' service day or something. So how about if I make a long weekend of it and come to see you? We can talk about it on the phone this weekend and..."

At that, Nicole let out an involuntary shriek that made

her miss the next part of the message. It also brought Brandon and Marissa running into the kitchen.

"What happened?" Brandon demanded eagerly. "Did you chop off your finger with a knife?"

"No." Nicole grinned at him. "No, nothing like that."

Soon Mr. Smith called the kids back into the other room and Nicole played back the message again, savoring the sound of Nate's voice. Two weeks! In just two weeks, Nate would be there with her!

Suddenly all lingering thoughts of Luc washed away in a flood of certainty. How could she even have worried that she might be starting to think of Luc as more than a friend? After hearing Nate's voice again, the very thought was completely ridiculous. The thing with Luc was just a silly, harmless flirtation. She and Nate were meant to be together forever.

Chapter Eight

From: PatriceQT@email.com

To: NicLar@email.com

Subject: Lucky Nate!

Hi Nic,

I heard Nate's coming 2 see u soon—2 cool! I'm soooo jealous (in more ways than 1, ha ha—Hank wouldn't even come 2 see me when I was sick last week cuz he was afraid he'd catch it! Hmmph. . . men!)

Anyway, hope the visit is great. Should b a good chance

for you 2 to reconnect & stuff. And in Paris, no less—oo la
la, très romantique! Lemme know what happens!

P

"Now *this* is what I call a house," Nicole joked, spinning on
her heel to take in the full view of the enormous, sumptu-
ous classical palace surrounding her on three sides.

Mrs. Smith smiled. "It's really something, isn't it?"

"Yeah." Nicole hadn't been particularly excited when the
Smiths had suggested a weekend day trip to Versailles, the
world-famous palace of seventeenth-century King Louis
XIV. She had originally intended to spend her Sunday
thinking about Nate. But his visit was still almost two
weeks away, and she figured this trip was probably as
good a way as any to distract herself so she didn't go crazy
with anticipation in the meantime. Besides, it would give
her something new and interesting to say in her Artist's
Eye class on Monday when Dr. Morley asked about everybody's weekend.

"I suppose you don't have too many places like the
château in America, eh?"

Nicole glanced at Luc, who was grinning mischievously at her. He had come along on the trip and was current-
ly standing with a Smith child hanging off of each arm.
Even though she still felt a little strange about her feelings
the other day, Nicole was glad he was there. They hadn't

had much of a chance to hang out or even talk in the past couple of days, and she sort of missed him. But just as a friend, of course.

They weren't having much luck talking here, either, though, as Luc was kept busy chasing after the rambunctious Smith kids. Nicole trailed along behind them, taking in the scenery as they entered the château and wandered from one sumptuously appointed room to another. It was a nice day and the place was crowded, with long lines everywhere. Nicole was pretty sure she'd heard more American voices within the first hour than she had since arriving in France.

And no wonder, she thought as she stared at an opulent tapestry. *I'm not surprised people come from all over the world to check out this place!*

Nicole was amazed by most of what she saw, from the richly decorated royal apartments to the gold-and-white royal chapel to the spectacular Hall of Mirrors. At first she kept mental notes, planning to write it all down in her journal later. But there was so much to see that after a while it was almost mind-numbing—so many paintings, so many gilded sculptures, so many velvet curtains and crystal chandeliers and columns and balustrades and vaulted ceilings, until she couldn't take in any more.

She was almost relieved when Mr. and Mrs. Smith suggested heading outside for a while. Soon they were all strolling through the extensive gardens surrounding the

palace, admiring the sculptures, reflecting pools, and well-tended shrubbery.

As they stopped to admire a particularly magnificent fountain, Nicole was getting more than a little impatient with the kids. When Marissa accidentally stomped on her foot, she decided it was time to get away from them, if only temporarily.

"Excuse me," she told Mr. and Mrs. Smith. "I'm going to try to find a bathroom. Be right back."

Whew! How does Luc do it? she wondered as she hurried off in search of the nearest restroom, which she really did need to use. *He has so much patience with those two, even when they're acting like total brats. And all I want to do is get away from them. Of course it will be a different story when Nate and I have kids of our own....*

She emerged from the restroom a few minutes later still enjoying a rosy fantasy about watching Nate cradle their future baby. When she arrived back at the spot where she'd last seen the Smiths, she found Luc alone, waiting for her.

"Where'd everybody go?" she asked him, glancing around.

"The children wanted ice cream." Luc stood up and smiled at her. "So I said I'd wait for you, and we would rejoin them later. For now, it is just us." He winked playfully.

"Oh well, I suppose I can put up with you for a little while, then," Nicole joked. But secretly she was pleased that he'd managed to arrange a little alone time for the two of them.

Just as friends, she reminded herself. But it would be nice to see some of the sights without the rug rats getting in the way.

The two of them wandered down the neatly tended garden path, weaving their way around tourists posing for pictures or ogling the elaborate topiaries and gurgling fountains. "So," Luc said casually after a moment. "Mrs. Smith tells me that your boyfriend, he is coming for a visit soon."

Nicole shot him a quick look, but his expression was neutral. "That's right," she said. "Nate is arriving a week from next Friday. I can't wait to see him!"

"Hmm."

Luc walked on for a moment or two in silence. Nicole's mind started drifting along in a pleasant fantasy of herself and Nate strolling together through a pretty garden like the one she was in now.

Then Luc spoke again. "I wonder if anything will seem different between you? After this time apart, I mean."

Snapping back to reality, Nicole shot him a sharp glance. "What do you mean?" she said. "We haven't been apart that long. It's no big deal."

"I'm certain you are right." Luc shrugged and smiled. "It's just that, some of the things I have heard you mention about him...Well, it is merely idle curiosity, that is all. As

you say, *ce n'est pas grand-chose*. And it is none of my business."

Nicole glared at him. "You got that right."

She couldn't believe he was using stuff she'd said about Nate to cast doubts on their relationship. Had she been a little too friendly to him lately? Was he starting to get ideas?

"You don't have to worry about me and Nate," she added firmly. "We may be apart right now, but a few months doesn't really matter when you have your whole lives in front of you."

"Okay, okay." He held up his hands in surrender. "I am sorry to bring it up. I meant nothing by it. Truce?"

Nicole shrugged. "Whatever," she muttered, still feeling irritated.

But Luc seemed ready to let the whole thing drop. "If we have time before we leave here today, perhaps we will visit the Hamlet." He waved one hand around to indicate some unknown place beyond the gardens. "It is a sort of make-believe village that Marie Antoinette had specially built for her on the grounds here at Versailles. There are several thatched cottages, barns, even a dairy where she kept cows. She used to visit and pretend to be living a simple, rustic life. I suppose it was her way of enjoying a type of life she would never choose for herself on a permanent basis. It is an interesting idea, eh?"

Nicole stared at him, puzzled by the sudden change of

topic. "Sounds a little weird to me," she muttered.

They walked on silently for a moment. Then, without warning, Luc suddenly stopped in front of a classical sculpture. "Ah..." he said under his breath, a knowing smile twitching around the corners of his mouth.

"What's with you?" Nicole asked, still feeling slightly irritated about his earlier comments. "You look like the cat who swallowed the canary."

"Eh?" Luc glanced at her, perplexed. "*Cat* I know of course, but what is the meaning of the word *canary*?"

"It's just an expression." She shrugged. "Never mind. You just look kind of strange, that's all I meant."

He nodded. "This place—it holds special memories to me." He waved one hand at the sculpture. "You see, it was here, before this very statue, where I shared my very first kiss with a girl, back when I was a mere boy."

"Really?" Nicole smiled, a little touched in spite of herself. "That's sweet. My first kiss wasn't anyplace this nice— it was in seventh grade, and this guy Mark got me in spin the bottle...." She trailed off, realizing her first-kiss memory seemed kind of lame, especially in this incredible place. "But anyway, that one didn't mean anything. The first kiss that really mattered was my first one with Nate."

"But does not every kiss matter?" Luc turned and gazed down at her, seeming genuinely interested in her answer. "It is always a moment of sharing something special— romance, friendship, fun, curiosity...."

Nicole shrugged. "I don't know," she mumbled, suddenly way too aware of how close he was standing...and also of how few people were in this particular nook of the gardens. "I guess I believe it's possible to separate the physical from the emotional."

That was something Zara liked to say, and Nicole smiled, pleased with herself for coming up with it. But Luc still looked serious.

"I see," he said. "Perhaps you would be willing to test that theory."

Before she realized what was happening, he cupped her chin in his hand, leaned down, and kissed her softly on the lips. For a moment she was too startled to react. Then he ran the fingers of his free hand up her arm and her whole body seemed to melt.

"No!" she blurted, pulling away, her heart pounding. What was she doing? "I—I can't do this!" she sputtered.

"C'était plus fort que moi," he murmured, reaching out to touch her arm gently. "I could not stop myself."

She brushed away his hand and hurried off, soon losing herself in the garden.

As soon as she was sure he wasn't trying to follow her, she flopped down on a park bench, breathless and flustered. "What a jerk," she muttered. What gave him the right to just kiss her like that? He knew she had a boyfriend— they'd just finished talking about him!

And what about you? a little voice inside her head queried. *What gave you the right to kiss him back?*

Nicole was still feeling guilty and confused when she and the Smiths arrived back at the apartment a few hours later. She'd managed to avoid being alone with Luc for the rest of the trip—now all she had to worry about was avoiding him for the rest of her stay in Paris.

Glancing up as Mr. Smith pulled the car over to the curb in front of their building, Nicole realized with a funny little jolt that she was happy to be back. It was a little alarming how she was starting to think of the place as home.

Maybe it would be best if I got out of here, she thought as she followed the Smiths up the steps. *Quit the program, went back home, and picked up midsemester there. After all, at this point Mom and Dad can't say I didn't give it the old college try.*

At the very thought of the word *college,* she shuddered, knowing she wasn't quite ready to face that conversation with her parents. But perhaps that wasn't the only reason she didn't want to go home early. Perhaps, on some level, she maybe, sort of didn't want to leave Paris just yet. She was almost starting to *like* it here.

How weird was that?

At least Nate will be here soon, she told herself. *Seeing him will definitely help put me back on track.*

Inspired by the thought, she flipped open her laptop, logged on, and pulled up a blank e-mail.

From: Niclar@email.com

To: N8THEGR8@email.com

Subject: visit

Dear Nate,

I can't wait to see you again! Two weeks is way too far away...

Being here just makes me more certain that you and I are meant to be. You know? It's like they say, I guess—absence makes the heart grow fonder.

I can't wait until I'm home again and we can go back to being together all the time. Then maybe we can start planning our future together, starting with college....

Speaking of college, did you decide where you're applying yet? As soon as you do, let me know so I can get the applications. Mom and Dad better not say anything about it, either. I've put in my time here in their little fantasyland mind-expanding travelogue, so now it's time for them to do some compromising, too. They're just going to have to realize that I know what I need to be happy, and that's being with you. That's way more important to me than which college I go to or what major I pick or whatever. End of story.

Anyway, we can talk more about that when you get here.
I'm counting the hours….

All my love,
N.

She sat back, took a deep breath, and read over what she'd written. It sounded a little rant-y and disjointed, but she shrugged and decided that didn't matter. Nate would understand. Leaning forward, she quickly clicked *send*.

Chapter Nine

From: N8THEGR8@email.com

To: NicLar@email.com

Subject: no subject

Hey Hot Stuff,

Glad yer so geeked out about my visit, lol. You should
be, baby, b/c ya know I'm not that thrilled about coming to
Le Croissantsburg—but you're worth the sacrifice, heh
heh. Still, ya better tell those Frenchies to stay outta my

way or I'll show 'em what a good ol' American linebacker
can do...

See ya soon,
N.

"Nicole? Nicole! Are you there?"

Nicole blinked, slowly becoming aware that Annike was
waving a hand in front of her face and peering at her with
a slightly aggravated expression. They were in the middle
of a cooking lab for their culinary-arts class—all around
them, other students were mixing, stirring, taste-testing,
chatting, and generally having a good time—but somehow
Nicole couldn't get all gung-ho about making a *gâteau au
chocolat,* which as far as she could tell, despite the fancy
French name, was just a plain old chocolate cake. She was
too busy just trying to get through the time remaining until
Nate's visit.

"Sorry," she mumbled. "Were you saying something?"

Annike rolled her eyes and muttered some words in
Swedish. "Only six times now," she added, "I asked you to
hand me the bowl with the egg whites and sugar in it."

"Sorry," Nicole said again, grabbing the glass bowl near
her elbow and handing it over. "Guess I'm a little distracted
these days."

"So I've noticed."

Nicole watched as Annike poured the butter she had

just melted into the bowl, then added flour. She tried not to let her mind slip back to the topic of Nate's visit, but it wasn't easy. There were only three days to go now, and the closer it got, the harder it was for her to think of anything else.

"Um...so did you and Petra have fun at the play last night?" she asked as Annike stirred the batter. Annike had gotten the three of them tickets to a new comedy playing at a local theater the evening before, but Nicole had backed out of the plans a couple of days earlier.

Annike glanced up at her before returning her gaze to the bowl. "Sure," she said. "It was really funny. Petra couldn't stop giggling for hours afterward. It is too bad you missed it."

"I know." Nicole smiled tentatively, wondering if Annike was mad at her for blowing off the play. "I just really wanted to get the homework for French class out of the way so I wouldn't have to worry about it this weekend. I don't want anything to distract me from spending every possible second with Nate while he's here."

"Right. I got that. Well, Chloe appreciated your ticket, anyway."

Nicole winced. Was it her imagination, or did Annike sound a little disapproving?

"I mean, Nate's only going to be here for a few days," she said, feeling a bit defensive. "Of course I want to make the most of it."

Annike shrugged. "Of course. Could you hand me that spoon, *s'il te plaît?*"

Yep. She's annoyed, Nicole thought as she handed Annike the spoon. She couldn't really blame her; she hadn't exactly been Friend of the Year material the past couple of weeks.

Part of her felt guilty about that; she didn't want to lose Annike's friendship. Then again, if Annike were a true friend she should understand how important Nate's visit was to her. Shouldn't she?

At that, her mind skittered back once again to Nate. She couldn't wait to see him—and to share Paris with him. Thanks in part to her Artist's Eye class, she had a long list of places they could go visit. The class had taken two more field trips in the past couple of weeks. Notre Dame, with its soaring interior and lurking gargoyles, had been impressive enough even to distract her from thoughts of Nate for a little while, though in the end she'd ended up imagining herself getting married in the ancient cathedral in a beautiful fairy-tale wedding. Just the day before, the class had visited the Jardin des Tuileries, one of the busiest parks in the city. Every time she saw a couple walking together, she felt an anticipatory pang. Soon, soon that would be her.

She wondered what Nate would think of that particular park. "I can't wait," she murmured, imagining the two of them strolling arm in arm through the neoclassical

gardens, stopping to kiss in the shadow of a topiary—

"What?" Annike asked rather sharply, looking up from struggling to whisk egg whites by hand while simultaneously keeping an eye on the pan of melting chocolate bubbling on the stove.

Nicole blinked, suddenly remembering where she was. "Nothing," she said. "Um, I mean, I'll give you a hand with that."

Somehow Nicole muddled through the rest of her classes that day. When she got home and checked her e-mail she found a message from Zara waiting for her.

From: ZZZar@email.com

To: NicLar@email.com

Subject: Coming soon to an airport near you...

Yo Nic,

Hope yer counting down the days til Nate arrives! I'm sure u already know this visit is totally key 4 u guys. This is the first time u've been apart 4 more than a few days, ya know? And it's no secret that boys have a short attention span. So make the most of it, girl! It's not every guy that would fly 2 a whole other continent just 2 see ya, so make sure u let him know he's worth it, too!

Anyway, have fun w/him, and don't do anything I wouldn't
do. (ha ha, as if!)

Luv ya,
Z

Nicole rolled her eyes and smiled. If she didn't know better, she might wonder whether Zara was a little jealous,
especially after that comment about not every guy being
willing to fly to visit. Zara had dated a lot of guys, but
somehow she'd never ended up with one special person
the way Nicole and Patrice had. She liked to pretend that
she preferred it that way—"use 'em and lose 'em," as she
put it—but sometimes Nicole wondered.

*Weird to think the great Zara Adams might actually envy
little ol' me,* she thought with a mixture of awe, pride, and
amusement. *Definitely weird.*

At that moment Luc knocked on the frame of her open
bedroom door. "Anybody home?" he asked with a smile.

"Oh! Hi," Nicole said. Up until then she had successful-
ly avoided being alone with Luc since the trip to Versailles.
"Um, hi."

"You said that twice." An amused smile twitched the
corners of his mouth. "So, are you busy? I was just going
to make some cookies with the kids. Thought you might
want to join us."

Nicole jumped to her feet. "Sorry," she said hurriedly. "I was just on my way out." She squeezed past him in the doorway, trying not to brush up against him. He didn't make a move to stop her as she rushed down the hall toward the apartment door.

As soon as she was outside in the hallway, she breathed a sigh of relief. It was going to be tough getting through the next couple of months with Luc right there in the apartment half the time.

But I can do it, she told herself as she headed for the echoing stairwell. *Especially after I see Nate this weekend. That will give me the strength to get through the rest of the semester. I mean, at least I'm sort of enjoying some stuff about Paris now.*

She smiled, remembering how shocked her parents had been when she'd admitted that to them during their last phone call. It was obvious that they were thrilled but also suspicious, as if they couldn't quite believe their plan had worked.

Not that it did, really, Nicole reminded herself. *I know they were hoping I'd get inspired to apply to, like, Harvard or the Sorbonne or somewhere instead of going to the same college as Nate. But they'll just have to realize that all the horizon expanding didn't change my mind about that. Even if it did show me that Paris is a pretty cool place.*

She was really looking forward to sharing some of that with Nate. She knew he didn't have the best attitude about

Paris—but then again, neither had she when she had arrived. Maybe this visit would give her just enough time to change his mind. In fact, maybe if she was successful, they could think about spending their honeymoon here someday.

Shivering happily at that thought, Nicole realized she'd reached the bottom of the staircase. She glanced at the building's front door, wondering if she had time before dinner to run down to the store to buy some American soda to have on hand for Nate's visit. Then she remembered that her wallet was still in her school bag upstairs.

"Je n'y crois pas!" she muttered, using a French exclamation Brandon and Marissa had taught her as she glanced up the stairs, trying to figure her odds of dashing in and out again without getting cornered by Luc.

As she was thinking, she heard a key jingle in the lock. Glancing around, she saw Marie attempting to open the door with one hand while juggling a bag of groceries in the other.

"Hold on! I've got it," Nicole called, hurrying forward to help.

"Ah! *Merci*, my dear," Marie said breathlessly when Nicole swung open the door. "You are a lifesaver."

Fifteen minutes later the groceries were put away and Marie and Nicole were settled in the parlor with cups of tea. Nicole had already told Marie about Nate's upcoming visit, but now she found herself telling the older woman all

about her specific plans for the weekend, the words pouring out of her so fast she was surprised Marie could follow them.

"Ah, it sounds most wonderful," Marie said after Nicole finished describing her plans to wind up Nate's first evening in Paris at the Eiffel Tower. "He is a lucky young man to have such a caring girl in his life."

Nicole shrugged. "No, actually I think I'm the lucky one," she said. "Sometimes I wonder what would have become of me if we hadn't met. But you probably know what that's like," she interrupted herself with a sheepish smile. "I mean, Renaud is pretty awesome, too. You guys must have made a totally cute couple when you were my age, right?"

"Well, not exactly." Marie took a sip of her tea. "You see, Renaud and I did not meet until we were both much older. We are married just nine years now, come December."

"Really?" Nicole blinked. Somehow, seeing Marie and Renaud together, she had assumed they had been together practically forever. "Wait, so what about before that? Were you married before?"

She immediately realized it wasn't a very tactful question. Luckily, Marie didn't seem offended. "No, in fact I was engaged once, when I was not much older than you. At the last minute, I realized it was for my family that I was getting married, not for me. After that I was—hmm—cautious of marriage."

"Sure," Nicole said, even though she wasn't.

"In any case, I was having a marvelous time and wasn't really looking for that sort of thing." Marie chuckled, her face taking on a nostalgic look. "Oh, I had boyfriends of course—quite a few, if I do say so myself." She shrugged and smiled. "I had no interest in children, so really I did not feel I was missing anything. By the time Renaud came along, I was ready."

"Wow." Nicole was still trying to wrap her mind around Marie's surprising revelation. "And you—you liked living like that? All alone?"

Marie chuckled. "Oh, *ma chérie*, but I was not alone. As I said, I had all the boyfriends I pleased. More importantly, I had wonderful friends and mentors and of course my family, always. Yes, I lived alone, but I was never lonely. There were always new things to do; it was as if there was not enough time in the world to do everything I wished. I traveled a great deal, I studied, I wrote and painted and even danced a little. Ah, though I adore my life now with Renaud, sometimes I am nostalgic for those carefree days...."

When she thought about it that way, Nicole understood a little better. It did sound sort of exciting in a way—being totally independent, able to do whatever one liked, whenever it struck one's fancy. Of course, having a true love to share it with sounded even better.

They moved on to talk about other things after that. But

when she left an hour later, Nicole returned to thinking about Marie's life story. How odd that a woman she'd thought of as so "normal" had such unusual ideas about things—things like marriage and children and happiness. As she trudged slowly up the steps toward the Smiths' apartment, the scent of warm cookies drifting toward her, Nicole tried to imagine spending all those years alone, never getting married or having kids, instead counting on painting or other pastimes to fill her life.

She shook her head. *I guess that sort of thing could be okay if that's how you happen to end up,* she told herself, quickening her step as the scent of the cookies tickled her appetite and made her stomach rumble hungrily. *But I'm glad I'll never have to worry about living my life like that.*

Chapter Ten

From: NicLar@email.com
To: Larsons9701@email.com
Subject: bonjour!

Hi Mom and Dad,

Not much time to write today; gotta get ready for Nate's
visit. And don't worry, I promise I won't try to smuggle
myself home in his suitcase (probably). Ha ha!

Love,
Nicole

"See you in Eye," Annike said that Friday at noon as she and Nicole parted ways outside their culinary-arts classroom.

Nicole stopped and turned toward her. "Oh! No, you won't, actually," she admitted. "I'm, um, taking the rest of the day off."

"What do you mean?"

"Nate gets here later today, remember?"

Annike rolled her eyes dramatically. "How could I forget?" she said. "It's the only thing you talk about these days."

Nicole grinned sheepishly. "Sorry about that." She wasn't really particularly sorry, though. After all, how could anyone expect otherwise under the circumstances? "But I hope you'll be able to meet him while he's here," she added. "Then you'll see for yourself why I'm so psyched to see him!"

"I would love to meet him," Annike replied. "Call me."

"I will," Nicole promised. "*Au revoir!* Oh, and if Morley asks where I am, just tell her I ate some bad sausage at the crêpe stand, okay?"

With one last wave—and a quick glance around for any teachers who might notice her departure—Nicole continued toward the doors. Soon she was outside heading for the *métro* stop.

She spent the next two hours browsing through some of the little shops she'd discovered in a neighborhood near the Île de la Cité. It wasn't even that she needed new clothes—Nate didn't care much about fashion anyway. But as the hour of his arrival drew closer, the thought of sitting in a stuffy classroom conjugating French verbs or discussing different ways to look at a streetlight was nearly unbearable. In the end, all Nicole bought was a pair of leather gloves as a gift for Nate. She returned to the Smiths' apartment feeling triumphant and happy.

I have just enough time to hop in the shower before I get dressed to leave for the airport, she thought, glancing at her watch as she pushed open the apartment door. *Then I'll get a cab and—*

She looked up from her watch and saw Luc standing in the hallway immediately inside the door.

"Your friend Nate just called," he said. "You are to call him back immediately."

Nicole stared at him, her mind not really processing this information. "Huh?" she said. "What are you talking about? I can't call him—he's on a plane over the Atlantic right now." She paused, her brain belatedly catching up with things. "Um, isn't he?"

Luc shrugged. "He said to call him at home. That is all I know."

Without another word, Nicole hurried past him, heading for the phone in the kitchen. What in the world was going on? She grabbed the phone, for once barely noticing the kids screeching in the next room.

Maybe the plane was delayed or something, she thought as her fingers flew through the international codes and then Nate's familiar number. *Or maybe something's wrong....*

"Yo," a very familiar voice answered on the third ring.

"Nate?" Nicole blurted out. "What are you doing there? Why aren't you here? What's going on? Is everything all right—are you sick? Did something happen?"

Realizing it might be useful to allow him enough time to respond, she forced herself to take a deep breath. On the other end of the line, Nate let out a little hangdog laugh—the one he always used when he thought she was mad at him.

"Sorry, babe," he said. "I know it's, like, kind of last minute. But I don't think I'm going to make it this weekend after all."

"What? Why not? What's wrong?" Nicole's mind was still filing rapidly through all the horrible possibilities—illness, death in the family, terrorist threats, broken bones....

"Don't make a huge deal about this, okay?" Nate replied. "It just didn't really seem like the right time, you know? I mean, you're over there doing your thing, I'm here doing mine...."

Nicole was so stunned that she was having trouble forming a coherent thought, let alone a meaningful sentence. "But—whu—I—" she stammered.

"Listen, I should hang up," he said before she could pull

herself together. "Dad's on my case already about all the major long-distance charges, you know? We'll talk later. Bye, Nic."

There was a click in her ear as he hung up. Nicole just stared at the phone in her hand for a moment, too stunned to feel anything. Then she heard someone coming into the kitchen.

"Everything is okay?" Luc asked.

His words broke through her daze like a hatchet through plywood, sending painful splinters flying every-where. No, everything was *not* okay. Not even close.

"Just leave me alone," she mumbled, racing past him and out the door.

Sometime later she found herself emerging from the *métro* stop near the Centre Pompidou and the Stravinsky Fountain. For a moment she wasn't quite sure how she'd ended up there—the time between leaving the apartment and arriving in that spot had been nothing but a blur of sadness, guilt, anger, and confusion.

Then she realized what she had done—she had auto-matically started the visit without Nate. This was to have been the first stop on his get-to-know-Paris tour. She'd imagined it so many times that her feet had taken her here even while her brain and heart were too busy short-circuiting to pay attention. Her stomach constricted painfully as she thought about how different her feelings would be if he

were there with her at the moment. They would have their arms wrapped around each other, still basking in the novelty of being together again and probably acting a little silly. She would point out the fountain, and then Nate would look up at the funky, colorful sculptures and say *Wow, that's pretty cool....*

Nicole shook her head, the fantasy shimmering like the ripples in the water beneath the spitting fountains. No, he wouldn't say that, she reminded herself. He'd probably say something like *Man, it takes a bunch of French freaks to call this kind of weirdo junk 'art.'*

She grimaced, her boyfriend's rude imaginary comments ringing in her ear. After all, Nate wasn't the type to appreciate anything too new and different.

Biting her lip, she did her best to return to the fuzzy, romantic version of her fantasy. There was no doubt he would be all over her at this point in her tour, weird sculptures or not. In fact, he would probably complain about having to wander around the city looking at stuff instead of just finding a handy spot for a nice make-out session.

Who cares about a bunch of freaky water-spittin' statues? he would say with that little half smile she'd always thought was so sexy. *I'm only here to see my girl anyway.*

She walked on slowly, looking around at the familiar plaza with a new awareness. Over the past couple of months, certain things had faded out of her consciousness as she got used to them. Things like the little dogs that accompanied their owners everywhere in Paris—and the dog poop they all too frequently left behind on the sidewalks, streets, grass, steps, and everywhere else. Nicole had become adept at watching where she stepped, but she could imagine Nate's reaction if he accidentally soiled one of his pristine top-brand basketball shoes in a stray pile.

He'd probably cuss at the top of his lungs for about ten minutes and then threaten to drop-kick any Parisian pooch that looked at him funny, she thought ruefully.

It wasn't just the dog poop, though. There were a lot of other things that had confused, annoyed, or otherwise bothered Nicole at first that she hardly noticed anymore. Such as the clouds of cigarette smoke that seemed to hang everywhere. Or the kamikaze scooters that dodged in and out of traffic and threatened to run people down on the sidewalks. Or the pervasive odor of urine that popped up at odd times even in the ritziest areas of the city. Even the irritation of not being able to understand most of the conversation going on around her or read the signs on the shops had faded as she learned more of the language.

When I got here I thought all those things were totally gross or scary or frustrating, she remembered. *When did that change?*

She sank down on a nearby bench, sending a small flock of roosting pigeons scattering. Her mind was spinning with uncomfortable new thoughts.

I guess my friends really set me up for that first impression of Paris, she realized, a little uneasy at the idea. *And maybe I set myself up for it, too. Okay, so maybe that was a little close-minded of me....*But now her opinions had changed, especially after hanging out with people like Annike and Marie and Luc.

Shaking her head and feeling vaguely disloyal, she wondered what that meant. Who was she, if she couldn't even form an opinion someone else didn't give her?

Just then a twentysomething couple strolled past. Their arms were intertwined, and the woman wore a single white rose tucked into her dark hair. Her companion— boyfriend, husband, lover?—was gazing at her with the kind of rapt adoration that made him look to be unaware that there was anything else in the world beyond her face.

Nicole's eyes filled with tears. Had Nate ever looked at her like that? All of a sudden she couldn't quite remember. But she knew it should be her strolling along the plaza, trading kisses and smiles, being happy.

She couldn't bear to sit there anymore. All she wanted to do was run home and spend the rest of her stay in Paris crying into her pillow. She rushed for the *métro* station, almost blinded by tears.

Chapter Eleven

Half an hour later Nicole was letting herself into the apartment as quietly as she could. But not quite quietly enough. Marissa's face popped into view around the corner.

"Nicole's home!" she shouted. Then she stepped forward. "Hey Nicole, wanna see what I painted?"

She held out one slightly grubby hand, which was holding a wrinkled sheet of construction paper. Forcing a smile, Nicole glanced at the picture painted on it. "Very nice," she said, trying to stay patient. "Who's that fat guy in the picture? Is that your teacher at school?"

The little girl looked surprised and slightly pained.

"Non!" she replied. "It's you. See your pretty blond hair?" She pointed at a streak of yellow at the top of the blobby figure.

Nicole was feeling desperate to escape. "Oh, okay, I see now," she said. "Um, it looks just like me! You're quite an artist."

"Thanks." Marissa shoved the paper toward her. "Here, you can have it if you want. Luc said we should be extra-nice to you today."

"He said what?" Without quite realizing what she was doing, Nicole accepted the picture. "Luc said that?"

At that moment Luc appeared. "Hey, Mari," he chided gently. "You were not supposed to tell her that."

The little girl shrugged and grinned. "Sorry." She skipped off, disappearing back around the corner.

Nicole bowed her head, not meeting Luc's eye. The last thing she wanted was his pity.

"Excuse me," she muttered. "I was just on my way to my room."

He caught her by the arm as she tried to pass. "Wait."

She blinked and stared down at his hand on her arm. "Let go," she said between clenched teeth. "I want to be by myself, okay?"

He dropped her arm immediately but made no move to retreat. "Are you sure about that?" His voice was unusually gentle. "I am here to listen if you like. I have been where you are myself. I think anyone who has ever loved has been there. I will try to understand—as a friend."

Nicole couldn't help being a little touched by his obvious concern. But she shook her head.

"Thanks," she said firmly. "But I know what I want."

The next morning Nicole woke up from a night filled with
restless dreams. But it wasn't until she glanced at the cal-
endar on her bedroom wall, the one with the big red heart
drawn around yesterday's date, that she remembered.
Nate. Nate wasn't here—wasn't coming.

The reality of it hit her like a Mack truck in the gut. It
was as if the entire universe had just rearranged itself,
leaving her feeling disoriented and slightly ill. The weekend stretched ahead of her, two endless days filled with
nothing but might-have-beens. With a groan, she dragged
herself out of bed and stumbled to her closet.

Why? she thought blearily as she pulled on a pair of
sweatpants and a T-shirt. *What did I do to make him
change his mind? Why wouldn't he want to see me?*

She stared around the small bedroom for a moment,
feeling lost. Then her gaze fell on her laptop. Maybe he'd
e-mailed her to explain.

Her heart jumped hopefully at the thought. Maybe this
was some kind of weird mistake. Maybe he just wanted to
switch the trip to next weekend or something....

Grabbing the laptop, she quickly logged on. The first
message in her in-box was from Nate. "Yes!" she whispered, clicking to open it.

From: N8THEGR8@email.com

To: NicLar@email.com

Subject: no subject

Hey Nicole,

    What's up? Look, I don't have much time 2 write. But this is important. I'm starting 2 think u and I might b taking things 2 fast, ya know? I've just been like, questioning stuff or whatever.

    Anyway, I guess this just isn't working 4 me anymore. So I think we should see other people. I hope we can still be friends.

    Nate

Nicole's heart froze as she quickly read through the message again, wondering if this was some kind of joke. He was "questioning stuff"? What did that mean? How could he say they were taking things too fast when they hadn't even been on the same continent for, like, *months*? And what did he mean, "see other people"?

Is he…breaking up with me? Her mind could hardly recognize the thought.

Leaving the computer blinking on her desk, she flew back out to the kitchen and grabbed the phone, her heart pounding. She tried Nate's number first, but there was no answer. She was about to try Zara, but she hesitated.

Somehow, Zara wasn't the person she wanted to hear this from. Instead she dialed a different number.

"Patrice?" she blurted into the phone when she heard her friend's chirpy voice on the other end of the line. "It's me."

"Nicole?" Patrice sounded startled. "Is that really you? Wow, how are you? How's Paris?"

"What's going on?" Nicole demanded without bothering to answer. "I just got a really weird e-mail from Nate. There's no answer at his house, and I need to know what's what."

"Um, what did he say?" Patrice asked weakly.

Patrice had never been a very good liar. Nicole could tell by her voice that she was being evasive. "What are you not telling me?" she cried. "Come on, Patrice, please! I need to know!"

"I'm so so sorry for not telling you this before!" Patrice wailed miserably. "Zara said I probably shouldn't get in the middle of it, even though I thought you should know, and you know how persuasive she can be when she thinks she's right—which is always, of course—and then Annie backs her up and it's like I can't stand up to them, and…"

"What?" Nicole practically shouted, clutching the phone tightly. "What didn't they want you to tell me?"

"It just happened last weekend." Patrice gulped loudly, clearly trying to regain control of herself. "We had the Harvest Dance, you know? Anyway, Nate went stag. But

then afterward...well, a few people saw him and Sherri Michaels out in the parking lot—you know."

Nicole felt her whole body go cold. "He kissed her?"

"Yeah." Patrice sounded sad. "He did. The rat."

The room seemed to swirl dizzily around Nicole as she tried to comprehend what she was hearing. It was true, then. Her whole life had just changed with one e-mail.

"He cheated on me," she said blankly, trying to make the words make sense. "He cheated on me, and now he's breaking up with me."

Just like you cheated on him, a little voice in her head accused pitilessly. She gulped. So far she hadn't told a soul what had happened between her and Luc that day at Versailles.

But she would deal with that later. Right now she had to fix this. Somehow, she had to put her life back on course.

I can't let this be the end of us, she thought in a panic. Everything she'd always counted on appeared to be slipping away. It was the scariest thing she'd ever faced—far worse than all those times her parents had announced they were moving yet again. Even worse than when they'd told her she had to go to France. Just when she thought she'd found her balance, something had come along to yank the rug out from under her feet.

Becoming aware that Patrice was still babbling away on

the other end of the line, Nicole suddenly snapped back to reality. Her friend seemed to be offering to tell Nate off for her the next time she saw him.

"No," Nicole interrupted numbly. "Don't do that. I—I think I'd better come home and straighten this out myself."

"Come home?" Patrice repeated. "Can you do that?"

"Sure, why not?" Nicole was already distracted, calculating the time difference between Paris and home and how long the flight would take. With any luck, she could be back there by midnight, Maryland time. "Look, I've got to go. I'll call you when I get there. Oh, and Patrice? Thanks."

She pushed the button to hang up, then prepared to dial again. But she immediately realized she had no idea how to go about booking herself a last-minute flight back to the United States. She stared at the phone in her hand, feeling helpless. The Smiths wouldn't be home for a couple of hours, and Luc was out somewhere with the kids. Besides, there was no way she was going to ask for *his* help with this....

"Marie," she murmured, suddenly hitting upon the answer. Marie would help her—she was exactly the kind of person who knew about this sort of thing.

Replacing the phone, Nicole hurried out of the apartment and down the stairs. She knocked sharply on Marie's door, hoping that someone was home.

A moment later the door swung open. "*Bonjour*, Nicole," Marie greeted her pleasantly. "What a nice surprise. Do come in and I'll put the kettle on."

"Thanks, but I don't really have time for tea today," Nicole told her. "I need your help with something. It's urgent. And superimportant."

Marie nodded calmly. "Well, come in anyway, and I'll see what I can do."

Nicole quickly explained the whole situation. Marie listened quietly as the words poured out of her.

"...and I'm afraid if I don't go home right now, he'll decide he made the right choice in that e-mail. But I know he didn't. He might think he wants to break up with me, but I know he doesn't really," Nicole finished at last. "He can't possibly realize what he's doing and what it means. That's why I need to get home as soon as possible."

"But why?" Marie challenged. "What will it accomplish?"

Nicole stopped, briefly annoyed. Hadn't Marie heard a word she'd said?

Then she thought about Marie's question. "Well, it will probably make my parents mad, for one thing," she admitted with a ghost of a smile. Now that she had slowed down a little, she realized that she and Nate weren't the only ones involved with this plan. "And I guess the Smiths will be sort of confused...."

"And you?" Marie prompted. "What about you? How will

it make you feel if you go and his mind does not change?"

"But what if I *can* change his mind?" Nicole argued, emotion swirling up in her again as she remembered what this was really about. "I mean, okay, maybe there are no guarantees or whatever. But how can I sit back and not even try?"

"Because it is his decision to make." Marie took both of Nicole's hands in her own and squeezed. "This is my point. He is feeling something, and whether you like it or not, it is perhaps not fair to try to change that. Do you see?"

"Not really," Nicole admitted. "I'm sure he's just confused because we're apart."

"Perhaps," Marie agreed. "And if that is true, he will come around when you return to him at the end of the semester, no?"

"I guess." Nicole shrugged. "Unless some other girl snags him before then."

"But if that were to happen, what would it say of his character?" Marie said. "Don't you think you deserve a boy who cares only for you—one whose head will not be turned by other girls?"

Nicole didn't know what to say to that. "So are you advising me not to go? To stay here and just stew about this?"

Marie smiled. "No. I am telling you to think about all your options before you act in haste."

That didn't seem like much help to Nicole. Suddenly she

felt very tired—too tired even to think about rushing around trying to book a flight that night.

"Maybe you're right," she said wearily. "I guess maybe I should sleep on it. I can always fly home tomorrow if I still feel like it."

"Yes." Marie lifted one hand and pushed back a lock of hair from Nicole's face, suddenly looking very maternal. "You always have choices, my dear. Always. Never forget that."

After saying good-bye, Nicole wandered back upstairs, still feeling confused and sad. The Smiths' apartment was still quiet and empty, making her feel lonely. She tried to call Nate, but got only his voice mail; she hung up without leaving a message.

Then she stared at the phone, wondering if there was any chance Annike might be home at the moment—and if she'd want to talk to her if she was. After the way she'd been acting the past couple of weeks, she wouldn't have blamed her if she didn't. But she really wanted someone to talk to, and she couldn't afford the long-distance charges to call her friends back home.

"Annike?" Nicole said tentatively when her friend's host mother called her to the phone. "Hi. It's me, Nicole. Are you busy?"

She was embarrassed to realize that her voice was quavering like crazy. Annike obviously noticed, too, because her voice was full of concern when she answered.

"No, I was just watching television," she said. "What's the matter? Is Nate there?"

"Not exactly." Nicole took a deep breath. "That's sort of why I'm calling...."

By the time she finished talking things out with Annike, Nicole actually felt a little bit better. But only a little.

It's nice to know I have true friends here, she thought, remembering Annike's sympathy and words of advice and commiseration. *But that doesn't change the fact that the love of my life just dumped me.*

Realizing it was way past lunchtime and her empty stomach was growling irritably, Nicole wandered out of her bedroom. She was surprised to find Luc waiting for her in the quiet, otherwise empty kitchen. "I thought you had the afternoon off today," she blurted out.

He shrugged. "I do. That is why I am here."

"Huh?" She was too tired and depressed even to attempt to figure that one out.

"I ran into Marie downstairs; I thought you might need company," he said. "The Smiths, they are out for a while taking the children to the park. So it is just you and me—you know, in case you want to talk. Or if you should want to take your mind off your problems and do something distracting."

Nicole's first, rather irritated thought was that he was trying to flirt with her and she opened her mouth, ready to shoot him down. Clearly Marie had told him about Nate.

But just because her boyfriend had dumped her, it didn't mean she was ready to jump into something with the next available guy she encountered....Then she looked at him and saw the sincere look in his green eyes.

She shut her mouth with a snap. "Is there any coffee?" she asked. "Or food? I'm starved."

"Right here." Luc bustled around the kitchen pouring her coffee, getting her toast and jam and a napkin.

The food and caffeine made her feel a bit better. But only a bit. It still felt as if her heart had been run over by a freight train. "Look, I appreciate the offer," she told Luc, who was leaning against the counter watching her eat. "But you don't have to waste your day off hanging around here. I'm not going to be much fun."

He fluttered one hand expressively. *"N'importe,"* he said. "I do not mind. Anyway, as I said, I think perhaps some distraction would help you. We could go out and do something."

Nicole tried to demur. But Luc just smiled and asked again. And again.

"Look, don't you have any friends of your own?" Nicole snapped at last, flicking a few toast crumbs off the table. "It's not that I'm calling you a loser, but it's a little weird how obsessed you are with this...."

Luc shrugged. "So we shall go out for a while, *n'est-ce pas?*"

Nicole sighed. It seemed he wasn't planning to take no for an answer.

"Whatever," she said wearily. "What did you have in mind?"

Luc smiled. "Why don't we go for a walk?"

A few minutes later they were wandering through the neighborhood, nibbling at crêpes from the local shop. It was a pleasant Saturday afternoon, and there were lots of other people out on the streets. The familiar hustle and bustle made Nicole feel a little more normal than she had all day.

She noticed they were approaching a popular local bistro. "I was going to bring Nate here for dinner last night." She shot Luc a sidelong, slightly suspicious glance, waiting for him to make fun of her or say something disparaging about Nate.

Instead he nodded. "It was a good choice," he said. "I am sure he would have loved it."

"I'm not so sure," Nicole muttered, scanning the menu board as they got closer. She wasn't really in the mood to defend Nate suddenly. "He'd probably complain about the menu being in French, then demand they cook him a cheeseburger or a deep-dish pepperoni pizza or something."

"Hmm," Luc responded.

Nicole bit her lip, suddenly feeling a little disloyal for her comments, true though they might be. "Of course there's

a lot more to life than food," she said hurriedly. "It's not like French food is exactly my favorite, either. Well, aside from crêpes and a few other things."

"Different people, different tastes—or as we might say here in France, *tous les goûts sont dans la nature,*" Luc said calmly. "Now, shall we go visit the Pompidou Center again? Or perhaps Notre Dame—a beautiful spot to go on a beautiful autumn day."

"Sure, whatever," Nicole said with disinterest, still staring at the menu board. She would have suggested that Nate order the *croque monsieur* or maybe the cassoulet. No matter how much he made fun of the names of the food, he would have had to admit it tasted good....

Maybe he'll change his mind about all this on his own, she thought with a sudden flash of hope. *Maybe that's what Marie was really trying to tell me—that he'll probably realize what he's done and that he misses me too much to leave things this way....*

That hopeful thought kept her occupied on the *métro* most of the way to Notre Dame. Luc didn't seem to have much to say for once, leaving her free to ponder it.

When they reached their destination and emerged blinking against the afternoon sunlight, Nicole's eyes turned immediately to the twin towers of the Gothic cathedral soaring toward the blue autumn sky. "Notre Dame. This was one of the places on my list to take Nate," she said. "I figured it's something he knows about, so he would probably think it was cool to see it in person, you know?"

Luc nodded. "It is a beautiful building. Much history." He laughed. "And then of course there are the gargoyles...."

"What's so funny about gargoyles?" Nicole asked distractedly, still lost in her own thoughts.

"When I was a small child, we had a—erm, what do you call it? School trip? In any case, we came here to visit as a class," he said. "When we went up to the bell tower, I went sneaking away from the group. I then sat crouched upon a bare spot pretending to be a gargoyle. When my teacher returned, very angry for my desertion, and tried to make me come with him, I did not move. After all, I was made of stone. How could I go with him as he asked?" He grinned. "Eventually the teacher had to lift and carry me back to the bus himself. He was very angry—all those steps...."

Nicole couldn't help laughing despite her mood. "That's cute," she said. "Did you get in trouble?"

"Not exactly." Luc shrugged. "My parents, they heard all about it from the teacher, of course. I think they found it funny. But to punish me, they made me play gargoyle on the front steps of our building. I squatted there for two hours, until my legs fell asleep." He grinned at her as she laughed again at the image. "See? Does not your heart feel better when you smile?"

Nicole's expression immediately reverted. "Give me a break," she muttered.

"Aha!" Luc cried. "That frown—it is exactly the one I wore upon my gargoyle face!"

He imitated her scowl, which made her smile again in spite of her problems. "Okay, okay," she said. "Very funny."

They wandered around through the gardens surrounding the cathedral for a while, not talking much. Just being there, with the chilly, fresh breeze blowing in off the Seine and the multilingual chatter of tourists all around her, made Nicole's problems seem a little smaller. She still felt a pang every time she thought of Nate. Was he hanging out with that bleached-blond little toad, Sherri Michaels? The very thought made her skin crawl.

But she also found herself distracted by Luc—and by Paris itself. There was a certain energy that always seemed to spark throughout the city like an electrical current. Sometimes Nicole found that energy exhausting. But that day, she was grateful for its demands.

The two of them climbed the hundreds of steps to the bell tower. By some chance there was nobody else up there except an employee, making the place feel a little like a private oasis in the busy city. As Luc looked out at the view, Nicole found herself staring at one of the gargoyles in particular, a grim-looking, hunched-over little fellow.

"You know, when you first look at that guy, he's totally

weird and ugly. But in a way he's actually kind of beautiful, too, isn't he?" she mused.

"Many things are like that, I think." Luc walked over and stood beside her, close enough that their sleeves brushed. "If one keeps one's eyes open, it is possible to see things in many different ways."

She glanced over at him with a smile. "Now you're talking like my Artist's Eye teacher."

He held her gaze. "Oh? Is that a compliment or an insult?"

Before she could answer, a group of tourists burst out of the stairwell, chattering away in what sounded like German. They swarmed through the tower, snapping pictures and consulting tour books as a harried-looking tour guide attempted to get their attention for a lecture.

Luc grabbed Nicole by the hand. "I think that is our cue to leave, eh?"

Nicole nodded and allowed him to lead her toward the stairs. They paused at the top, allowing a couple of stragglers from the tourist group to climb the last few steps, and Nicole closed her eyes for a moment, pretending that the hand she was holding belonged to Nate.

But it didn't work. She opened her eyes, pulled her hand away, and started down the steps.

"Come on," she called to Luc, trying to ignore the tears that were threatening to fall. "I think I need a cup of coffee."

Chapter Twelve

From: ZZZar@email.com
To: NicLar@email.com
Subject: Thisnthat

Hey Nic,

So do you still speaka the English, or are you completely Frenchified by now? LOL, j/k. Patrice told me what you
said in yr last e-mail to her about passing your midterm or
whatevah, and I'm still in shock. Who knew Nicki Larson
would be able to wrap her little mind around a whole

'nother language?

Anyway, keep the faith, girl. but don't forget where ya come from!

O, and 2 bad about Nate. Don't worry, he'll prob'ly get over it by the time u get home.

Z.

From: anniegood@email.com
To: NicLar@email.com
Subject: hi girl!

heya nicki-girl,

sorry i haven't writen much lately. how r u doing?

i have been dating a new guy his name is Phil. did z tell u about him yet? he is in college and studying 2b a phisy-cist (sp? i dont know how 2 spell n-e-thing w/o u here 2 help me! come home soon or im going 2 fail english this yr!! he he!)

so whats new w/u? write back soon,

luv,
annie

Nicole sighed and deleted Zara's e-mail without bothering

to respond. She clicked *save* on Annie's, even though she wasn't really in the mood to hear more chirpy news about her friend's latest admirer. Almost a week had passed since Nate had dumped her, and Nicole was getting annoyed by the way none of her friends even seemed to remember that it had happened. Sure, they had all been sympathetic at first. But after a few e-mails, it was clear that Zara had started to consider the matter old news. Aside from Patrice, Nicole's friends had barely mentioned Nate since then.

It's not them I should be mad at, she reminded herself, staring moodily at the computer screen and kicking at the leg of the tiny desk in her bedroom. *Nate's the one who did this to me, not them. He's the one who's still being a coward and avoiding my calls, not answering my e-mails....*

Still, she couldn't help letting a little of her annoyance spill over onto her friends. What gave Zara the right to make fun of her for learning French? "She's the one who practically flunked out of Spanish last year," Nicole muttered under her breath, brooding over her friend's e-mail. "If it wasn't for me helping her write that essay..."

Nicole sighed. She needed to stop letting Zara get to her. Her friend didn't know everything about everything even if she liked to pretend she did.

It was a thought that never would have crossed her mind three months earlier. Back then Zara had been the most worldly person she knew. But now...

She shook off the thought, reminding herself that it didn't really matter. When she got home she could share what she'd seen and learned in Paris with her friends—maybe help to open their minds a little bit.

But first, she had to get through this crisis. And apparently she was going to have to do it without her best friends. It was a depressing thought, and she decided it was time to distract herself from thinking about it.

Clicking off her computer, she glanced at the school bag she'd slung over the bed frame. She had vocabulary lists to memorize for French class, problem sets to do for calculus, and she really needed to write in her class journal before she forgot everything she'd seen on the latest Artist's Eye field trip to the Catacombs.

But she wasn't in the mood for homework at the moment. Somehow, reading her friends' messages had left her feeling more restless and unsettled than ever. She wandered out of her room, wondering if it would be rude to drop in at Marie's apartment for a chat so close to dinnertime. Or maybe she should just go for a brisk walk through the neighborhood....

She was still trying to make up her mind as she stepped into the front hall just in time to see Luc pulling on his leather jacket. His book bag was at his feet and Nicole could hear the sound of the Smith kids chattering at their mother in the kitchen nearby.

"Oh! Are you leaving?" Nicole asked Luc.

He reached back to straighten his collar. *"Oui,"* he said. "I was just thinking of going for some dinner. Would you like to join me? It is my treat, of course."

Nicole only hesitated for a second. "Sure," she said. "That sounds cool."

Luc looked surprised but pleased. *"Bon...génial*—that would be very cool. Shall we go, then?"

Nicole was already wondering if she was being an idiot. What would Nate think if he knew she was going out on a dinner date with another guy?

She shoved the guilty thought aside. Why would he care? He'd broken up with her, after all.

Besides, it wasn't really a date—despite Luc's offer, she would make sure to pay for her own meal just so that remained perfectly clear. She and Luc were friends, nothing more, and she planned to make sure things stayed that way. This was no different than going out for pizza with Patrice back home.

That settled it. Not only was she going to go, she was going to do her best to forget all about Nate for a little while and have a good time. She needed the break.

"Okay," she told Luc. "Just hold up while I tell Mrs. S where I'm going...."

A few minutes later they were heading for the *métro* station. "I know we could eat here in the neighborhood, but I want you to try my very favorite bistro in Paris," Luc told Nicole as they walked. "It is rather close to your

160

school, I believe. If you like it, you can go there with your class friends, *d'accord*?"

"Sounds good," Nicole said. "I need to find some new places to eat over there. The crêpe guy is starting to look at me funny 'cause I'm there so much."

When they reached the restaurant in question, Nicole had to admit that it was charming. The place was small and cozy, with burnished dark wood and gleaming brass everywhere. Several of the people working there seemed to recognize Luc, including a couple of pretty young waitresses.

"My, my," Nicole teased in a whisper as they took a seat at a table near the window. "You certainly seem to know all the hot chicks in Paris."

"You mean those girls?" Luc shot the closest waitress a disinterested glance. "What need have I of looking at other girls? I have the prettiest girl in Paris sitting across from me already."

Caught by surprise at the compliment, Nicole blushed. She was searching her mind for a witty comeback when she heard someone call her name. She looked over her shoulder and saw Annike waving from a nearby table.

"Hey, there's my friend Annike," Nicole told Luc. She saw that Annike was sitting with one of the Australian girls from their Artist's Eye class, the dark-haired, birdlike Janet. "Oh! And Janet, too. Let's go over and say hi."

"Isn't it funny to see you here?" Annike called with a

smile when Nicole approached her table. "Janet and I looked for you after class to see if you wanted to come with us. But you were already gone. Perhaps you read our minds!"

Janet giggled and nodded. She and Annike were both casting curious looks at Luc, who was right behind Nicole.

Nicole glanced back at him. "Oh, this is Luc," she said, suddenly feeling awkward, as if she'd been caught in some kind of clandestine affair. "He's my host family's nanny. Um, and my friend," she added.

Annike and Janet introduced themselves. "Why don't you two join us?" Janet suggested brightly. "We haven't even ordered yet—everything on the menu sounds so good we can't make up our minds!"

"Oh, if nothing else, you must try the *pommes frites*," Luc said. "They are easily the best in Paris."

Soon they were all sitting at a larger table in the corner. As Nicole unfolded her napkin she cast a sidelong glance at Luc, who had ended up sitting across from Annike.

Annike laughed at something Luc had said. Luc smiled back at her. She was looking particularly lovely that evening—her blond hair was slightly windblown and the aqua-colored sweater she was wearing set off her clear blue eyes. Her long, slim legs were equally flattered by her short black skirt.

Story of my life, Nicole told herself ruefully. Now Luc would surely turn all of his attention to Annike. Even Nate, if he were here, would be doing the same thing—checking out Annike's legs while pretending he wasn't.

But to her surprise, that didn't really happen. While it was clear enough that Luc admired the Swedish girl's beauty, he spent as much time talking to the much plainer Janet as he did to Annike. And whenever he caught Nicole's eye, he seemed to have a special smile or a wink just for her.

The four of them barely stopped talking long enough to eat the delicious food that Luc ordered for them. They discussed the girls' classes, Luc's college courses, travel, politics, sports, music, and just about every other topic under the sun. Normally, Nicole wouldn't have felt comfortable contributing much to the conversation, but for some reason her shyness seemed to have disappeared. She spoke up eagerly, arguing playfully with Annike over which of them was the worse French cook in their culinary-arts class and discussing France, fashion, and philosophy with Janet and Luc.

Even after they'd eaten every scrap of food on their plates, they sat there for a long time over cooling cups of coffee. Finally, though, Janet glanced at her watch.

"Sorry to shoot through so early," she said reluctantly. "If I don't rack off soon, my host family will likely call out a search party."

As she started to stand up Luc jumped to his feet and pulled out her chair. "*À la prochaine*—until we meet

again," he said. "I always assumed that Nicole would have charming friends. Now I know it is true."

Blushing slightly, Janet grinned. "Too right, mate!"

"I should go, too." Annike took one last sip of coffee. "I have heaps of homework to do tonight."

"Ugh! Don't remind me." Nicole groaned. "Oh well, even if I'm up till morning doing it, this was fun."

"Definitely! You should bring Luc along more often." Annike smiled at him. "*Au revoir*, guys. Nicole, see you tomorrow."

"Bye." Nicole watched them go, then glanced at Luc. "We should probably hit the road, too. It's getting kind of late."

Luc sighed. "I suppose you are right," he said. "But maybe we have time for just a short walk first? To help us digest."

Nicole knew she should say no. It really was getting late—at least if she wanted to get even half her homework done. But she wasn't quite ready for the pleasant evening to end yet.

"Well...okay," she said, relenting. "Maybe a short walk isn't such a bad idea."

They strolled along the street side by side, hands buried in their jacket pockets against the chilly night air. There was no moon, which meant the only light came from the buildings around them and the tall streetlights, which cast

their pale yellow glow upon the sidewalk and divided the whole scene into light and shadow.

"So how did you like the girls?" Nicole asked, breaking the comfortable silence that had fallen between them since leaving the restaurant.

"They are both very nice," Luc replied. "Very intelligent, too. You have good taste in friends."

Nicole smiled at the compliment. "So," she added casually, "Annike is awfully beautiful, isn't she?"

Luc glanced over at her. They happened to be in a shadow between streetlights at the moment, so his expression was difficult to read. "Of course," he said. *"Qui se ressemble s'assemble."*

Nicole pursed her lips. "What does that mean?"

They stepped into the next puddle of light, and Luc stopped and turned to face her. "Ah, your French is so much improved lately, I forget you do not speak it as a native."

Nicole blushed. "Thanks. So what does it mean?"

"It is a French proverb. It says in English, erm, 'Those who resemble, assemble.' I think another way you might say it is 'Birds of a feather, they will flock together.'"

"Oh!" She knew he was exaggerating a little—nobody with two functional eyes would ever say she was as beautiful as Annike. Still, it was nice to be flattered.

A sudden flash of anger washed over her. Nate might

throw around the occasional "beautiful" or "hot stuff" or whatever, but how often did he actually pay her a sincere compliment, one he had to think about a little?

Not very often lately, she realized. *Not for a long time, come to think of it.*

"Come," Luc said over his shoulder, moving down the sidewalk. "I want to show you something. It's just ahead."

Nicole hurried after him, still brooding over Nate's behavior. She was so deep in thought that she almost bumped into Luc—he had stopped rather abruptly at the next corner.

"Look," he said softly, pointing over and up.

Nicole followed his gaze. There, rising in the air, so close it seemed almost larger than life, was the angular metal skeleton of the Eiffel Tower. White lights picked out its every curve and strut, making it stand out against the dark sky.

"Oh!" she gasped in surprise. "It's—it's beautiful!"

She had seen the Eiffel Tower many times, of course—it was difficult to go anywhere in the center of Paris without coming upon yet another view of it. But from this angle it looked like a whole new structure, looming and strangely mysterious, almost alive.

Becoming aware that Luc was watching her rather than the Tower, she turned and met his gaze.

He smiled. "I thought you would appreciate it," he said.

"You, I think, have the ability to see what is special, what is important."

His face moved closer. Nicole stared into his eyes, mesmerized by the guileless, undemanding appreciation she saw there. So different from the way Nate looked at her most of the time.

She did nothing to stop Luc as he bent down and kissed her. His lips felt soft and warm against her own, and she let her eyes fall shut as she pressed against him.

Nicole was still shaking a little as she let herself into her room forty minutes later. She flopped on her bed and stared up at the ceiling with no thought for the homework that still awaited her.

"Idiot," she hissed at herself. "You're such an idiot!"

She still couldn't believe she'd done it again. Her mind raced, trying to make sense of it. What was wrong with her, anyway? No matter what was going on between her and Nate at the moment, she wasn't ready to write him off completely just yet. And that meant she had no excuse for kissing Luc again. One time might be excused as a mistake, just a silly impulse in a weak moment. But twice?

She shuddered, remembering the way her arms had snaked around his neck and pulled him closer. What might have happened if that noisy taxi hadn't come along the quiet street and interrupted them? Would she still be

standing there kissing him without a second thought for her boyfriend of two years?

Okay, so technically they were broken up at the moment. That didn't mean she should be throwing herself at any guy who came along. Not if she ever wanted them to have a chance to work things out... The guilt was so overwhelming she wasn't sure she could stand it.

But maybe the guilt was good, she decided. It would be there, strong and bitter, reminding her to control herself from now on. Reminding her just what was at stake.

Because there was no way she was going to risk everything she ever knew she wanted for some silly Paris fling.

Chapter Thirteen

From: NicLar@email.com
To: PatriceQT@email.com
Subject: Deep thoughts

Hey Patrice,

It's me. It's weird to think that you guys r all running around getting ready for Txgiving. Nobody here cares about it at all. I don't even get the day off from school! :(

I'm still not sure what to do about N. I emailed him a coupla more times, but he only wrote back 1x. And he

didn't really say anything. I guess he's not ready to talk about it.

My friend Annike thinks I should move on with my life and see what's what when I get back. But I dunno. Maybe things with N weren't as perfect as I thought. We had a good thing going (as U know!) but he isn't very good at communicating. When we get back together we'll have to work on that.

Hope things r good w/u + Hank. Happy turkey day.

Nic

Nicole tilted her head back, doing her best to take in the soaringly beautiful, light-filled, iron-and-glass central hall of the Musée d'Orsay. The museum, a former railroad station, was the site of Dr. Morley's latest class trip. The students had broken up into small groups to wander around taking in the architecture and the artwork, which included sculptures by Rodin, Impressionist masterpieces by Monet, Degas, van Gogh, and Renoir, and much more.

"So?" Annike said, wandering over to stand at Nicole's side. "What do you think? This has always been my favorite museum in Paris, ever since I first visited with my family as a little girl."

"I can see why," Nicole said. "It's gorgeous. And I love this kind of art."

Annike nodded. "You know what else is gorgeous?" she asked playfully. "The south of France. So did you think about it? Are you coming with us?"

Nicole glanced over at her with a weak smile. "Um..."

Annike had been bugging her for the past few days about a trip she was planning for the upcoming weekend with Janet, Ada, Petra, and Chloe. She wanted Nicole to come along.

At first Nicole hadn't even considered it. She had too much on her mind, what with the whole Nate situation. But now, after all of Annike's wheedling and pleading, she wondered if she should just give in and go—if nothing else, maybe it would take her mind off her problems.

"Come on," Annike cajoled. "You have to decide soon; it's Wednesday already, and we're leaving first thing Saturday. Anyway, you know you want to. It will be fun!"

"I don't know." Nicole wandered along the gallery without really seeing the artwork in front of her. "You're talking about Thanksgiving weekend, and I don't think they celebrate Thanksgiving in Nice."

Annike rolled her eyes. "They don't celebrate it here in Paris, either, silly."

"Well, the Smiths might have something planned, or..." Nicole didn't bother to finish. It was a pretty weak argument and she knew it. "I guess you're right. It could be fun. I'll ask the Smiths if it's okay with them."

"Yay!" Annike cheered happily. Her voice caught the attention of Ada and Janet, who were looking at a painting nearby.

The Australian girls hurried over. "What?" Ada demanded eagerly. "Did you talk her into it? Is she coming?"

Nicole couldn't help smiling at her enthusiasm. "Yeah, I guess I'm coming," she said.

"Bonza!" Janet exclaimed happily. "You'll see, we'll have a great time."

Annike smirked. "Oh, and if you wanted to ask a certain someone along..."

"You mean Luc?" Nicole wrinkled her nose. "You know we're just friends. Barely even that, really."

She felt a little sad as she realized that was becoming all too true. More than a week had passed since that kiss in the shadow of the Eiffel Tower, and so far she was upholding her vow to be good. That meant staying away from Luc as much as possible, at least whenever they might possibly wind up alone.

But it's all for the best, she told herself as her friends moved on to the next exhibit, chattering happily about their trip. *It's definitely all for the best.*

When Nicole got home that afternoon, Mrs. Smith was in her office. The twins were napping in their crib nearby and the older kids were nowhere to be seen or heard, which probably meant they were out with Luc.

Mrs. Smith looked up with a smile as Nicole entered. "Well, hi there," she greeted her. "How was school today?"

"Fine," Nicole replied. "I have something I wanted to ask you."

"Shoot. I'm listening."

Nicole quickly explained about the weekend trip Annike and the others were planning. "If you don't think it's a good idea for me to go, that's totally okay," she added hastily. "I mean, I don't want to put you on the spot or..."

Mrs. Smith chuckled. "Don't be silly, Nicole," she said. "It sounds like a lot of fun. Of course you can go, as long as you get your parents' okay."

"Great. Thanks." Nicole wasn't sure whether to feel happy or nervous at the permission. "I guess I'll call Annike and tell her."

Annike was thrilled by the news. "Oh, we're going to have such a blast!" she exclaimed. "I can't wait."

"Me, either." Annike's enthusiasm was catching, even over the phone, and Nicole couldn't help smiling. "So I guess we can talk about the details in school tomorrow. *Au revoir.*"

"So what are you girls planning to do down there in the southlands?" Mr. Smith asked, leaning across the table to help himself from a dish of mashed potatoes.

Nicole finished chewing her bite of turkey and stuffing. It was Thursday evening and the Smiths had prepared a

traditional American Thanksgiving dinner. It felt a little strange to be celebrating the holiday, knowing that almost no one else in Paris probably even knew it was today. But it was sort of nice, too. It made the Smiths feel almost like part of her real family. Of course that hadn't stopped her from feeling more homesick than she had in a long time while talking to her parents on the phone earlier....

"I'm not sure," she said in answer to Mr. Smith's question. "Annike found us a cheap hotel down in Nice, so I guess we'll just start there."

"If you can, you should try to get over to Monte Carlo," Mrs. Smith said, glancing up from feeding one of the babies a bite of strained peas. "It's quite a lovely city. All of Monaco covers only one square mile, but such a fascinating history!"

Mr. Smith grinned. "Right," he said. "And it's a whole separate country, so you can add it to your travel tally."

"My tally is pretty pathetic so far," Nicole admitted. "A total of three, if you count the time my parents took to Mexico when I was like a year old."

"That's nothing!" Brandon looked up from his mashed potatoes, which he appeared to be forming into a scale model of the Eiffel Tower. "I've been to twelve jillion countries!"

"You have not." Marissa frowned at him. "You've been to the same number as me. That's, um..." She glanced toward her mother for help.

"Seven, sweetheart," Mrs. Smith said calmly, scooping a

bit of greenish goo off the baby's chin. "America, Canada, France, Spain, England, Belgium, and Italy."

"Wow. You guys have been to all those places?" Nicole asked.

"With the children." Mr. Smith nodded. "Lynn and I have been to quite a few others as well. We honeymooned in Africa and spent our first anniversary in Fiji—ah, those were the days, weren't they, dear?"

As the couple smiled nostalgically at each other across the table, Nicole shook her head in amazement. Nobody she knew traveled like that. Even her parents had visited only four or five foreign countries. None of her friends had been anywhere, except for Patrice, who had relatives in Canada.

I guess that really does make me the worldly one of the bunch, she mused. *Weird.*

The thought almost made her drop her fork into her potatoes. Her, Nicole Larson—worldly? It didn't compute. Zara and Annie were the sophisticated ones in their group; always had been. The two of them had practically created an art form out of making fun of Nicole's inexperience and náiveté.

Nicole shook her head again, amazed at the ways this trip was forcing her to see things differently. But was she just developing a more sophisticated way of seeing, as Dr. Morley might put it—or was the trip actually changing her? Turning her into a different person? The idea was sort of scary.

• • •

The next morning Nicole was standing in the kitchen sipping at a cup of coffee when Luc entered.

"Oh!" Nicole glanced around, feeling trapped. So much for staying out of his way.

"Good morning," Luc greeted her cheerfully, seeming unaware of her consternation.

She was already preparing to push past him on her way out of the room. "Excuse me," she said. "I have to go."

Luc raised an eyebrow, moving to block her way. "Was it something I said?" he asked playfully.

Even though he was joking, she decided to answer honestly. After all, he deserved that much—he needed to know why they weren't going to be able to hang out anymore.

"Listen, I need to talk to you about something," she said. "Um, I like you. You're a really cool guy, and you've been a good friend to me. But I really need for us to cool it from now on. You know—not hang out or whatever. With this whole thing with Nate, I just can't deal with you right now."

"But why?" Luc tilted his head to one side, looking befuddled. "What is this about, Nicole? I do not understand."

She bit her lip, feeling a little embarrassed. "It's just—well, the flirting and stuff. The—the kissing. It's not fair to continue with that sort of thing. Not if I want to work it out with Nate. I just need to keep things clear in my own head, you know?"

Luc shook his head. "Ah, but it was always clear to me that you are devoted to Nate. And I respect that. I only wanted to be friends with you. At this point in my life, I have no time for anything more."

Nicole blinked in surprise. "Huh?" she blurted out. "Then why did you kiss me?"

Luc chuckled. "Why not?" he said. "I wanted to kiss you, so I did. You did not seem so upset at the time."

"That's not the point." Nicole frowned at him. "If you only wanted to be friends..."

"Relax. You are thinking too hard about this, eh? We are young; this is a time for both of us to have fun, to enjoy each other's company. Whether or not that involves kissing...well, it is okay either way."

Nicole took a step back, completely confused. "But you were the one who said every kiss matters."

"Did I?" Luc seemed amused by the comment. "Yes, that sounds like something I might say. But all I meant was exactly that. The kiss itself matters. Because of course it does. But that doesn't mean it has to be part of something larger, or so serious."

At that moment they heard a shriek from the direction of the nursery.

"Uh-oh," he said. "It sounds like it is time for me to go to work. Are we okay now?"

"Sure." Nicole shrugged, still confused. "I guess."

With one last smile he hurried out of the room, leaving her alone with her muddled thoughts. On the one hand, a lot of what he'd just said made sense. But could it really be true? Could a kiss sometimes just be a kiss—nothing more, nothing less?

Why can't things just go back to normal? she wondered with a depressed sigh. *If I'd never come to Paris, I wouldn't have to worry about any of this....*

Chapter Fourteen

From: Larsons9701@email.com

To: NicLar@email.com

Subject: Your weekend trip

Nicole,

Happy Thanksgiving! It's strange not to have you here with us for the holiday. We miss you. Dad and I are still so happy that you're going to Nice with your friends this week-end. We're glad you're giving this travel thing a chance. Be

sure to take lots of pictures, and send us a postcard if you can find the time among all the fun!

Love,
Mom

"Nicole? There you are!"

"Here I am." Nicole forced a smile. She still felt kind of strange about going off on some weekend jaunt when so many things in her life were so uncertain. "Am I late?"

"No. I just got here myself." Annike beamed at her and reached out to give her a hug. "This is going to be so much fun, isn't it? I'm so glad you decided to come. After all you've been through with your boyfriend lately, you probably really need the break."

"Thanks." Nicole was touched by her concern. "I just hope I don't bring everyone down. I'm not in the greatest mood these days, as you know."

Thanks a lot, Nate, she added to herself with a sharp twinge of bitterness.

Annike waved one hand in the air as if to brush aside the concern. "Never mind," she said. "We'll cheer you up. Besides, it will be good for you to get out and about. You shouldn't sit home and mope, right?"

"True." Nicole grimaced. "I'm sure Nate isn't sitting home alone moping over me."

"Hush," Annike said sternly. "Don't think about that. If

180

you do, you're letting him control your happiness. You deserve better than that."

Nicole sighed. "I guess you're right."

Even though she was pretty confident that she and Nate would get back together, it was difficult just to sit back and wait for that to happen. She still wondered if she should have allowed Marie to change her mind about flying home right after Nate broke up with her. Was she just letting someone else run her life again, as she'd lately realized she'd often done with Zara and Nate?

When we get back together, things are definitely going to be different. As in, way different, she promised herself with another flash of bitterness—or was it anger? *I'm not going to let him push me around anymore. And if he ever pulls anything like this breakup crap again—well, let's just say it won't be pretty....*

Becoming aware that Annike was smiling sympathetically at her, she forced a smile in return. This weekend was supposed to be about distracting her from her problems, not dwelling on them.

"Um, can we talk about this later?" Nicole asked. "I'd kind of like to forget about it all for a while."

"Of course." Annike grabbed the duffel bag out of Nicole's hand and slung it over her own shoulder. "We should get going, anyway—our train will be leaving pretty soon."

They headed across the platform to where the rest of

their little group was waiting. Nicole greeted Janet, Petra, and Chloe.

"Now if Ada ever gets her arse out here, we'll be all set," Janet commented with a yawn, glancing at her watch. "Hope she didn't oversleep. She hates getting up this early!"

As if on cue, a tall, gangly blur of pale skin and freckles rushed toward them, long limbs flying in all directions. "I'm here, I'm here!" Ada cried cheerfully. "Don't let the train leave without me!" She skidded to a stop. "Oh! Cheers, Nicole. You're with us after all! Annike kept saying she was afraid you'd back out."

"Hey! You weren't supposed to say anything," Annike protested, shooting Nicole a sheepish grin.

Nicole laughed. "Okay, it's scary how well you know me," she said. "Now come on—all aboard before I change my mind!"

"Whew! It's nice to finally get off that bloody train and stretch my limbs," Ada commented as the girls disembarked on the platform in Nice.

Nicole nodded, setting down her bag and stretching her arms over her head. She had spent big chunks of the five-plus-hour journey staring out the window, brooding about Nate. She wondered if it had been a mistake to come on this trip.

The other girls gathered around. "This place is supercool!" Janet proclaimed, slinging her duffel bag over her shoulder, looking around eagerly. "Come, we should find our hotel quickly. I'm hungry! It is past time for lunch!"

Nicole couldn't help smiling at her enthusiasm. They crowded into two taxis and were soon checked into their hotel, a bare-bones but spotlessly clean place. Their two spacious adjoining rooms were crowded with a hodgepodge of single and double beds and little else except an extra door that Nicole first thought must lead to a closet. But when Janet opened it, she discovered that it was actually an in-room shower.

"Ace!" Janet exclaimed. "I thought the dunny would be out in the hall."

"It is, I think," Annike replied, peering at the sign on the inside of the shower door. "This is just a shower, not a toilet. Looks like it requires change if you want hot water, too."

"No worries." Janet shrugged. "Still better than expected, eh?"

As she dropped her bag on one of the beds, Nicole could only imagine what her friends back home would say about it. *Not exactly the Ritz, is it?* Zara would snark. Patrice would probably try to make the best of it, pointing out the clean-swept floor and the high ceiling, but Annie would just bite her lip and stare sadly at the shower. *You mean we have to go wandering halfway down the hallway every time we have to pee?* she would whine.

Nicole shuddered, a little glad they weren't here. Then she caught herself. They might not be experienced world travelers or perfect in every way, but they were still her best friends in the world. And she'd be crazy to think she wouldn't rather be with them right now....

"Excuse me!" Janet pleaded as the others continued to poke around the rooms. "Lunch, remember?"

"Oh, right." Annike glanced at her watch. "It's getting a bit late, isn't it? Maybe we should skip the restaurant thing for now." At Janet's horrified squeak, she smiled and held up one hand. "No, I don't mean to skip past lunch. I only mean we could go to *l'épicerie*, buy some food there, and eat outside—it's such a lovely day, after all. And it will be faster."

"Good idea," Chloe agreed. "*Un morceau de fromage, un litre d'eau minérale,* and I'm ready to go."

"Everybody agreed, then?" Ada glanced around. Nicole nodded along with the others. "Okay, let's go!"

With a little help from the hotel staff, the girls soon located a nearby grocery. They bought cheese, bread, mustard, fruit, bottled water, juice, soda, and anything else that looked good. They emerged from the store loaded down with bags.

They headed straight for the beach, which was only a few blocks from their hotel. Nicole was surprised to discover how rocky it was—it was nothing like the sandy beaches back home in Maryland. But she soon found that sitting on the pebbly surface could be surprisingly comfortable. In any case, she forgot all about it as she reached for a crusty loaf of French bread.

The girls ate until there was nothing left. As Nicole licked a bit of mustard off her fingers, she sighed with pleasure as she glanced up and down the curving, hotel-lined coastline. She realized she hadn't thought about Nate at all for at least half an hour. The idea made her feel a little confused and uneasy, almost as if she were doing something wrong.

Oh well, she told herself, lying back on the rocky ground and closing her eyes against the intense Mediterranean sun. *Nothing I can do about that now….*

They all lay there on the beach for a while resting and digesting. The weather was really too chilly for sunbathing, but it was still much warmer than it had been back in Paris. There weren't many other people lying in the sun, but a few strolled along the shoreline or sat in beach chairs reading or napping.

"Anyone fancy some sweets to top off?" Chloe said after a while.

"Ugh! How can you think of eating anything more?" Petra groaned.

Nicole opened her eyes, shading them from the sun with one hand. "I could go for dessert," she said. "Do you think they have crêpes here?"

"Je ne sais pas," Chloe said.

Leaving Annike, Petra, Janet, and Ada behind, the dessert seekers walked up to the promenade. Nicole was watching for a crêpe stand, but before she had time to find one, Chloe let out an excited shriek.

"There!" she cried. "They have gelato!" She pointed toward a small street cart.

"What's gelato?" Nicole asked.

"Oh, it's brilliant," Chloe responded with enthusiasm. "It's Italian ice cream. Totally delish!"

The two of them hurried toward the cart and began scanning the handwritten menu board. "Can you believe it?" Chloe exclaimed when they joined her. "The menu is in French, not Italian!"

Meanwhile Nicole stared at the menu board, trying to decide which flavor to try. She would have preferred crêpes, but Chloe seemed so enthusiastic about the gelato thing that she didn't want to say anything. Trying something new wouldn't kill her, right? Besides, the gelato did look pretty tasty.

"*Fraises*—that's raspberries, right?" Chloe mused beside her.

"No." Nicole glanced over at the other girl. "Raspberries would be *framboises*. *Fraises* is strawberries."

"Oh! Cheers, you saved me, then." Chloe shuddered. "I don't fancy strawberries at all."

As Chloe pondered her berry choices, Nicole ordered

herself a hazelnut gelato. When she tasted it, she was glad she had. It was delicious.

The girls spent the rest of the weekend seeing the sights in and around Nice, gorging themselves on French food and pastries along with the occasional gelato, walking on the beach and the promenade, visiting the outdoor market, and generally having a great time. Nicole managed on more than one occasion to stop thinking about Nate for hours at a time, though she also had long periods during which she felt horrible, adrift, angry, and uncertain about the future.

Luckily, during those times she found a sympathetic listener in Annike. "I just do not think one can change other people," Annike said as the two of them took a twilight stroll along the promenade one evening. "It is for him to decide what to do."

"I know." Nicole sighed. "And I'm sure he'll still want to be with me in the end. It's just so hard to wait around while he figures that out, you know?" She hesitated. "Besides, now that this has happened, it's sort of making me wonder...."

Annike glanced over as Nicole's words trailed off into silence. "What?"

Nicole shrugged.

"It's just—sometimes I wonder if it's worth it," she said

quietly. "I've spent the past two years assuming Nate and I would be together forever. *Wanting* that. And now..."

"You aren't sure you want that anymore." It was a statement rather than a question, which immediately put Nicole a bit on the defensive.

"No, not really," she said quickly. "I mean, of course I still love him. That's the important thing. I'm probably just being silly because I'm so pissed off at him right now for cheating on me. That's all. This will pass, and things will go back to normal."

Even as she said it, she couldn't help wondering if she was kidding herself. *Is Nate worth all this angst?* she thought with a flash of irritation—at him, and also at herself.

Annike didn't say anything for a moment. "Come," she said at last. "We'd better try to find the others if we still want to go dancing tonight."

Nicole nodded and followed her as she headed back through the narrow, crowded streets of Nice toward their hotel. But her mind wasn't on their evening plans.

Instead she found herself thinking seriously about Nate—both his good points and his shortcomings. He wasn't Mr. Perfect, that was for sure. She'd always known that. He was impatient and distractible and always late, he wasn't the most intellectual guy in the world, he could be thoughtless and maybe a little selfish at times. But she'd always accepted those faults as a part of who he was, a sort of balance for the sweet, kind, surprising, impulsive, funny elements of his personality. No, he might not be perfect, but she'd always thought he was perfect for her.

But was he really? And if he wasn't, what would she do about it?

Chapter Fifteen

To Nicole's surprise, returning to Paris after the weekend trip felt a little like coming home. The late-afternoon sunshine reflecting off the puddles outside the train station, the constant background scents of baked goods and gas fumes in the streets, the solid facades of the buildings she passed—even the screeching Smith kids seemed familiar and comfortable as she entered the apartment.

After greeting the Smith family, she headed for her room to check her e-mail. When she fired up her laptop, she found messages from both Zara and Patrice. Her heart jumped into her throat when she saw that there was also a new message from Nate. She clicked it open immediately.

From: N8THEGR8@email.com
To: NicLar@email.com
Subject: no subject

Hey Nic,

It's me again. Look, I've been thinking about us some more. Maybe I was too harsh before. We had a pretty good thing going, and it's just this stupid France thing that's getting in the way. And that's yr parents' fault, not yrs—I know u don't want 2 b there any more than I wanted u 2 go... So anyway, I want 2 try 2 work it out when u get back. What do u say?

Yours if u'll have me,
N.

Nicole read through the message at least six times, hardly daring to believe her eyes. Could it be true, or had she finally snapped and started seeing things that weren't there?

Still feeling a little stunned, she clicked on Patrice's message.

From: PatriceQT@email.com

To: NicLar@email.com

Subject: news

Hiya Nicole,

Okay, maybe you won't want 2 hear this, but I think I should tell u: Sherri M. just dumped Nate. I don't know all the details yet but I'll keep u posted. I just thought you'd like 2 know… And he totally deserves it 4 what he's put u thru. Even Hank sez N's a snake, and u know he doesn't have very hi standards, lol…

Hang in there, sweetie,

Patrice

For a second Nicole felt deflated. So Nate hadn't just decided this on his own, then. His new flame had ditched him, so he was running back to her.

I know what Annike would say about that, and Marie, too, she thought. *They'd tell me I was too good for him and should be glad he's out of my life. That I shouldn't take him back even if he begs.*

She could see their point, too. Why should she take him back just because his tacky little fling hadn't worked out? It would be like getting *doormat* tattooed across her fore-head in big red letters. He'd treated her like total crap, and now here he was, expecting her to forgive him and pretend nothing had happened.

She took a few deep breaths, trying to control her anger. It worked—she managed to stop focusing on what Nate had done and move on to what he was offering. She had her future back! Suddenly life looked much easier than it had just a few minutes earlier. It seemed all she had to do was survive her last few weeks in Paris and she could go back to her real life—it would be there waiting for her after all.

Hitting *reply*, she typed in "Dear Nate," then sat there for a moment with her hands poised above the keyboard. She realized she didn't know what to say to express how she was feeling. It seemed important to let him know just how momentous this was—how very close they had both come to having their lives changed forever, and how lucky they were that now that didn't have to happen. But she also wanted him to know how angry she was and how much he'd hurt her. With all of these mixed emotions running through her head, the right words wouldn't come.

Oh well, she could let him sweat it out for a while, she decided at last, closing the message box and clicking *don't save*. She'd write back to him in a while when she'd calmed down. After all, he deserved it after what he'd put her through.

Realizing she hadn't looked at Zara's message yet, she clicked on it.

From: ZZZar@email.com
To: NicLar@email.com
Subject: Go get 'im!

Hey chica,

P. just told me about Nate+Sherri going bust. That didn't take long, eh? U should write 2 him and let him know you're ready to hear him beg 2 come crawling back 2 u. Act like it's a maybe thing, tho—of course u aren't going 2 say no, but he doesn't have 2 know that! ha ha!

Anyway, better act now. Don't give him another chance 2 do something stupid. U def. don't want 2 let this 1 get away, esp. over some lame trip to Croissantland.

Z.

"Ugh!" Nicole exclaimed with a grimace. Leave it to Zara to make her feel like the world's most predictable loser. That did it. She had to get out and think for a while—everything just seemed to be hitting her the wrong way somehow, and it was starting to freak her out.

Nicole rushed out of the apartment, barely pausing long enough to throw on a jacket. Halfway to the *métro* station she slowed from a brisk walk to a crawl, wondering if she was making a big mistake. Maybe she shouldn't wait to answer Nate's e-mail. What if Zara was right and he changed his mind in the meantime? Glancing over her shoulder, she wondered if she should go back.

No, she decided. He would just have to wait for her this time. Lord knows she'd waited around for him often enough in their time together. Mr. Twenty Minutes Late, as even his own mother jokingly called him. Nicole didn't want to look back and feel as if she'd rushed this decision.

She sank down onto a convenient park bench. She could say no. For the first time, she really realized that—and thought about it. Did she really want to go back to Nate now? Suddenly she wasn't sure. She wasn't sure at all. She thought about the past months in Paris—all the new things she'd learned, the new experiences she'd had, the new friends she'd made. Did she really want to pretend all that had never happened, that she was still the same old person with the same old hopes and plans?

On the other hand, if she walked away from her relationship with Nate, it meant admitting once and for all that her longtime dreams weren't going to come true. What did that mean for her future?

The question made her uncomfortable, and she hopped to her feet again. She needed to go somewhere that would let her think, somewhere familiar and peaceful and safe....

A short while later she found herself at Notre Dame. Most of the tourist crowds were gone, leaving only a few people strolling the grounds or feeding the pigeons. The cathedral itself glowed in the crimson rays of the setting

sun, and just seeing its ageless facade made Nicole feel a little calmer somehow.

She closed her eyes as a breeze wafted in off the Seine and ruffled her hair. Although she had intended to think seriously about the future—particularly her future with Nate—she found her mind wandering off in the opposite direction. Had it been only a couple of months ago that she had first arrived in Paris, anxious and nauseated and certain she could never survive a whole semester in a foreign country?

But it didn't really feel that foreign anymore, Nicole realized, opening her eyes and looking around. She really was starting to feel...at home here. She never would have believed that was possible.

Then again, she'd done a lot of things she never would have believed she could do. In fact, she'd probably done more new things and thought more new thoughts in her few months in Paris than in the seventeen years before that. Everything from living with a strange family to learning to speak French to the trip with her new school friends.

Thinking about the Nice trip reminded her that Annike and the others were already talking about going somewhere together over the winter school break. At the moment they were still trying to decide between Switzerland and Spain.

Nicole realized she was a little sad that she wouldn't be joining them, since she was leaving for home just before

Christmas. Who would have believed it? Her, wishing she could do more traveling? It was like she was turning into a whole different person....

Noticing that dusk was rapidly approaching, she stood and stretched. That was the trouble with the future—it was so hard to know what might happen. Maybe she was asking too many questions, expecting too much. Maybe it would be easier to wait and try to figure it all out when she got home. Sure, she was mad at Nate right now—that was only natural after what had happened. But seeing him again might clear up her doubts.

For a second the thought comforted her. She could go back to the apartment and e-mail Nate right away—tell him she wanted to try again, too. Tell him that she forgave him, that they were meant to be together, that nothing had changed.

Then she glanced up at the majestic spires of Notre Dame and shook her head. Sure, she *could* do that—put off her own questions and doubts, seek sanctuary in the familiar, let all the rest slide for a while and just see what happened. The trouble was, she knew better. If the past few months had taught her anything, it was to look and see and question in ways she never had before. She had Dr. Morley's class to thank for that, and Luc, and the Smiths, and Marie, and Annike. Not to mention Paris itself. And maybe herself, too.

• • •

Nate picked up the phone on the second ring. "Nic!" he exclaimed when she identified herself. He sounded happy to hear from her, though he also sounded a little distracted. "Yo, it's great to hear your voice. Listen, can I call you back tomorrow, though? I was just on my way out."

"This won't take long." Nicole took a deep breath. She wanted to do this now, while the clarity she'd found at Notre Dame was still fresh in her mind. "I got your e-mail, Nate. And I've been thinking about it a lot."

"Yeah?" Nate still sounded distracted. "That's cool. I'm glad we're seeing eye to eye on this. And I'll make it up to you for putting you through it, trust—"

"No, wait," Nicole interrupted. "The thing is, I—I don't think it's going to work. Us, I mean." Her eyes were already filling with tears, but she did her best to keep her voice steady. "I think you were right the first time. We should break up."

"What?" This time she could tell she had his full attention. "Listen, babe. You're talking crazy here. Why don't we just play it by ear for now, talk it out when you get home and figure out what to do...."

"No." She kept her voice as firm as possible without being mean. "I've made up my mind. I'm breaking up with you."

There was a long moment of silence. "Fine," Nate said at last. His voice sounded wounded and a little surprised.

"If that's the way you want it. But you'd better make sure—it's not like there aren't plenty of other girls who'd love to take your place."

"I know. And I'm sure about my decision." Nicole squeezed her eyes shut. "Good-bye, Nate."

She waited for a few seconds to see if he was going to answer. When she heard him hang up, she set down the phone and burst into tears.

It wasn't going to be easy. But even through her sadness, she was already pretty sure it had been the right thing to do.

Chapter Sixteen

From: Larsons9701@email.com

To: NicLar@email.com

Subject: Welcome home (soon!)···

Nicole,

Dad and I can't wait to see you! It's hard to believe that the whole semester has already passed. As I've written before, we've been missing you like crazy. But even though it's been hard being without you, we're so happy that the semester abroad has worked out so well for you.

Sorry to hear about Nate. We can talk more about that when you get home if you want.

Enjoy your last few days in Paris, thank the Smiths for us, and travel safely!

Love,
Mom

"...and so I would like to finish by saying that I cherish young Nicole as a dear friend, and will miss her terribly." Marie raised her glass, waiting for her audience to do the same.

Nicole shyly raised her glass. The Smiths' living room was packed with people. More than a dozen of Nicole's friends from school had come—Janet, Petra, Ada, Chloe, even Seamus and Finn from her Artist's Eye class. The entire Smith family was there, of course; Luc was distracting the two older children by bouncing them on his knees on the sofa, and the babies stared wide-eyed at the gathering from their playpen.

"And finally," Marie finished her toast, "as tribute to our friend Nicole's experiences here in Paris, I will say to her that she reminds me of one of my favorite French proverbs: *À coeur vaillant rien d'impossible.* That means, nothing is impossible to a valiant heart."

Her listeners applauded, then raised their own glasses to their lips. Nicole took a drink, then surreptitiously

swiped at her slightly teary eyes with her free hand. Marie's speech had followed equally nice ones by Mr. Smith, Annike, and several others. It was truly touching to realize that so many people would miss her when she left the next day.

"I saw that, you old softy," Annike whispered teasingly in her ear.

Nicole turned and smiled at her. "I must have something in my eye," she joked. Then she glanced around. "A lot of people came, didn't they?"

After a moment someone started calling for Nicole to make a speech. The others joined in, and soon she realized she really should say something. She *wanted* to say something.

Stepping to the front of the room, she cleared her throat, feeling only a twinge of nervousness as all eyes turned toward her. "*Bonsoir*, everyone," she began. "Thanks for coming to my farewell party, and thanks a million to the Smiths for throwing it. They've been so nice to me this whole time—they didn't have to do this, too. But it's awesome to have all my new friends here in one spot." She smiled. "It's funny to think that when I came, I couldn't imagine I would make any friends here. After all, what could I possibly have in common with a bunch of French people?"

There were chuckles from her audience. "Hey, we are not all French, you know!" Petra called.

Nicole grinned at her before continuing. "But anyway, I guess I figured out that I have more in common with you than I thought. I'm proud to call you all my friends. And since Marie finished her speech with a French proverb, I want to do the same. This is one I learned from Luc." She smiled in the direction of the handsome young nanny, who looked surprised and curious. "It goes, *qui ne risque rien n'a rien.* He who risks nothing has nothing. He first said it to me, like, two weeks after I got here. He was trying to talk me into going out to dinner with him at the time."

She grinned as most of the females in the room shot knowing and amused looks in Luc's direction. He held up both hands in surrender.

"Anyway, when I first learned what it meant, it didn't make that much sense to me," Nicole continued. "But now I understand it a lot better. I have all of you to thank for that. So *merci pour tout.* And I won't say good-bye, but rather *à bientôt*—until we meet again." She lifted her glass and smiled as everyone clapped.

"Thank you, Nicole," Mrs. Smith called out. "It's been an honor having you here—you've become a member of the family." She turned her smile to include the rest of the room. "Now, I want all of you to feel that same way. Please make yourselves at home and enjoy the delicious food, most of it provided by our dear neighbors Marie and Renaud and also by Nicole and her culinary-arts class-mates. *Bon appétit!*"

A few minutes later the visitors were happily eating, drinking, and mingling. Brandon and Marissa were helping Luc pick up used cups and napkins and carry them to the trash bin in the kitchen.

They're really not such bad kids, Nicole mused as she watched them from a distance, nibbling on a pastry. *They're just kids. I guess maybe I expected them to be something they aren't. But I think I'm actually going to miss them—at least a little.*

Just then Annike peeled away from a little cluster of students near the food table and walked over. "Nice speech," she said with a smile. "Hard to believe you are really the same girl who could hardly say a word in front of a class without turning red and forgetting how to speak English, let alone French."

Nicole grinned, thinking back to that awkward day in their Artist's Eye class when she'd had so much trouble describing the *métro.* "I know. My friends back home probably won't recognize me."

The comment came out sounding more wistful than she'd intended. Annike looked sympathetic. "Are you worried about what your friends at home will say?" she asked.

"A little." Nicole stared down at the pastry in her hand. "I mean, it's not going to be easy to face Nate again. I don't think he understands why I didn't want to get back together with him." Tears sprang to her eyes, but she swallowed them back quickly. "But I had to do it. He wasn't right for me, no matter how many times my friends told me he was. And no matter how much I wanted him to be."

Annike nodded and sipped at her drink. "It will get easier," she said softly.

"I know. That's one thing I've learned this semester, at least." Nicole smiled ruefully. "Anyway, at least Mom and Dad are pretty psyched about the new me."

Annike giggled. "Could they talk to my parents?" she joked. "When I told them I wanted to travel to America to visit you next summer, they nearly passed out at the thought of the plane fare."

"Don't worry, we'll find you a good deal." Nicole grinned. She could hardly wait to show Annike around her world. "Maybe you can even talk Petra or some of the others into coming along."

"I'll start working on it when we go to Spain next week," Annike promised. "I think Petra really wants to meet your friend Patrice—she cannot believe you know someone else who talks as much as her!"

Nicole chuckled. "It will be a meeting of the motor-mouths."

She was still thinking about Patrice—and her other friends back home—as someone called Annike, leaving Nicole standing alone again. At around the same time she'd decided she really didn't need a boyfriend like Nate

anymore, Nicole had also started to realize that she didn't need—or want—Zara's bossiness in her life anymore. It was scary to think about pulling away from Zara, especially since it meant she would surely lose any hope of friendship with Annie as well. Where would that leave her next semester?

With Patrice, she thought fondly. Patrice had been the only one to e-mail with sincere concern and sympathy after hearing she'd broken up with Nate for good. That was a true friend.

They'd need each other to face the Wrath of Zara the next semester. But Zara would just have to realize that if she still wanted to be friends with them, it would have to be on their terms. And if she didn't? It didn't really even seem like such a big deal now that Nicole had so many other things to look forward to.

Despite the courage of her thoughts, she shivered a little. It wasn't going to be easy. But what was?

"Are you cold?" a voice spoke behind her. "I can shut the windows."

Turning, she saw Luc standing there, for once free of the children. He was holding a wineglass and smiling, looking just as handsome as he had the first time she'd seen him. Only now he also looked like a friend.

"No, that's okay, I'm fine. Just thinking," she told him.

"Looking forward to going home?" he asked.

"Sort of." Nicole gave him a half smile. "I mean, of course I can't wait to see my family and everything. But some of the other stuff…"

He nodded. She had already told him what had happened between her and Nate.

"There will be a lot of changes for you. But many of these changes are good, *n'est-ce pas*?"

"You're right, they are. I'll be busy next semester figuring out exactly what I want to do next year. Where to go, whether I want to stay in one particular place or travel around more, whether to take classes again or maybe get a job. And of course after that, there's college to consider. I was so sure I'd be following Nate to school that I've barely even considered my options." She shrugged. "Anyway, it's all pretty scary to think about, but exciting, too. And I think I can handle it as it comes, you know?" She wrapped her arms around herself. "Who knew I had this brave, adventurous person inside of me?"

"I think your parents knew it," Luc pointed out. "That is surely why they sent you here." He winked. "And I knew it, too. Who else but a true adventurer could come up with such a haughty brush-off of my advances immediately after vomiting all over the sidewalk?"

Nicole winced, knowing she would probably never live down her not-so-grand entrance to Paris. But that was okay, too.

"Well, you guys were smarter than me," she said. "Because if I hadn't come here, I'm afraid I might never have figured it out. At first I wasn't even sure I'd be able to survive here. It all just seemed really, really hard, you know?"

He sipped at his drink. *"Oui,"* he said. "But as we French might say, *il faut casser le noyau pour avoir l'amande.*"

"You have to break the shell to get the almond?" Nicole translated uncertainly. "Oh! I get it—it's sort of like saying 'No pain, no gain!'"

"See? You are now understanding French almost like a native." He raised his glass and smiled. "A toast to you, and to the unknowable future—*les jours se suivent et ne se ressemblent pas.*"

"Thanks. And thanks for being *un vrai ami*—a true friend." Nicole returned his smile, feeling proud of herself.

It was true what she'd said to Luc—if she hadn't come to Paris she might never have figured out all of this important stuff. She might have gone ahead with her plans, followed Nate to college and then married him, settled for a predictable, totally unexamined life...and that was way scarier than anything Zara, Nate, or the next year might throw at her.

Now, instead, she found herself looking forward to more great adventures like her semester in Paris. She was even looking forward, sort of, to telling her parents that she wanted to put off college to travel for a year.

Somehow, she had a feeling that they wouldn't have a problem with that.

I think they'll like the new me, she thought, glancing around at the people who represented the rich, interesting, independent life she'd made for herself in Paris. *I know I do. And I can't wait to see what the future holds for me.*